I0581790

THE DOOR

THE DOOR

A NOVEL

CATHERINE MCDAUGALE

The Door

Copyright © 2025 Catherine McDaugale

www.CatherineMcDaugale.com

Published by Wild Lily Books (an imprint of Walk By Faith Media, LLC)

Littleton, Colorado

ISBN: 978-1-956509-08-3

Unless otherwise indicated, all Scripture quotations are from the New King James Version. Copyright © 1982 by Thomas Nelson, Inc. Used by permission. All rights reserved.

Any internet addresses in this book are offered as a resource. While all links are active at the time of publication, because of the dynamic nature of the internet, some web addresses or links contained in this book may have changed and may no longer be valid. They are not intended in any way to be or imply an endorsement by Wild Lily Books, and Wild Lily Books cannot vouch for the content of these sites for the life of this book.

All rights reserved. No part of this publication may be reproduced in any form, stored in any retrieval system, used by AI learning models, or transmitted in any form by any means—electronic, mechanical, photocopy, recording, or otherwise—without the prior permission of the publisher, except as provided by United States of America copyright law and fair use.

Author photo: Aaron Lucy

Printed in the United States of America

For Mattie:
Thank you for sharing
life's adventures with me.

CHAPTER 1
1991

Seven-year-old Anna froze when she saw a strange man dart out of her house and up the street. Until then, it had been a normal Monday. She didn't realize that her life would soon be irrevocably different.

Her mind was preoccupied with the stuff a second-grader thinks about. On the school bus, she tried to remember if her spelling word, *tomorrow*, had two m's or two r's. She spoke the word slowly to hear if it *sounded* like it had two m's. It did. But it also sounded like it had two r's.

She got off the bus a stop early to go to Sarah's house. Her friend hadn't been at school. Sarah's mom told her Sarah had a cold.

As she crossed the street to go home, she wondered why everyone called her family's two-story house "the Mansion." Although big, it wasn't *that* big. She had seen houses much larger than theirs. But the stones did make it look like a castle. It was the first built in the area, long before the others.

She noticed the different shades of red leaves on the tree in the front yard: scarlet, crimson, and burgundy. Just last week, her mom taught her those names. The red leaves stood out against their drab background.

And then it happened. As she pondered the different colors, the front door opened. A man with long and unkempt dark hair emerged. His pale face starkly contrasted with the darkness of his scraggly beard. Anna had never seen a beard down to the middle of a man's chest. What was he doing in her house?

Even his black pants and white shirt looked odd. She couldn't tell exactly *why*. But they did. His clothes were unlike anything she'd ever seen her dad wear.

The man glanced to his left and right, leaped down the steps, and ran away.

As Anna tried to make sense of it, a car honked. She flinched and realized she was standing in the middle of the road. When she looked again, the man was gone.

Anna hurried across the street. When she reached the other side, she stopped. What should she do? She squished her eyebrows together. Who was the man? And why did he leave the house like that? Were there others?

She decided to go to their neighbor's house first. Mrs. Garwood would know what to do. Anna ran up the steps to the porch and rang the doorbell. She breathed in the crisp autumn air, shivered, and pulled her jacket tightly around her.

"Hi, Anna dear." Mrs. Garwood smiled and dusted the flour off her apron.

Mrs. Garwood's cat, Simon, walked to Anna and purred. Anna picked him up and looked at Mrs. Garwood. Her hair was pulled back into a loose chignon at the nape of her neck. A few white strands stood out among her chestnut brown hair.

"It's so good to see—" Mrs. Garwood wrinkled her brow. "Are you okay? What's wrong?"

"I'm scared." The quiver in her voice surprised her. "I just saw a man with a creepy beard run out of our house."

"Come in. Let me put on my shoes, and we'll go see what's going on."

Anna held Simon close and followed Mrs. Garwood inside.

THE FRONT DOOR was ajar when Anna and Mrs. Garwood got to her house. Emboldened by Mrs. Garwood's presence, Anna pushed it open and called out for her mom. She rushed to the kitchen and saw her mom's purse on the counter. Her keys hung on the hook by the door, and her shoes were on the shoe shelf. She opened the garage door. Her mom's car was parked inside.

Anna ran through the back door onto the porch. The oak tree loomed, but there was no sign of anyone. She called out again as she searched the backyard. Besides the crunch of the russet-colored leaves underfoot, her call was met with silence.

Mrs. Garwood waited on the back porch. She put her arm around Anna. "Come inside and sit on the couch. I'll go look upstairs."

She let Mrs. Garwood guide her.

"Sit here, and I'll be right back."

Hot tears streamed down Anna's cheeks as she listened to Mrs. Garwood's footsteps on the stairs. They grew distant as she searched the rooms. But then she heard the floorboards on the stairs creak and knew she was returning.

"Your mom's not upstairs. Hold tight, I'm going to look in the basement."

Anna fidgeted, clasping and unclasping her hands as she waited. Then she heard the basement door close.

"Your mom's not here. Let's call your dad."

Anna walked to the red phone on the wall, dialed her dad's work number, and handed the phone to Mrs. Garwood.

"Hi. Is Jim there? Okay, I'll wait." Mrs. Garwood smiled reassuringly at Anna. "Hi, Jim. It's Lydia. I'm here with Anna, and she's home alone. Can you leave work early?"

Anna looked expectantly at Mrs. Garwood.

"Okay, good. I'll wait here with her." Mrs. Garwood hung up the phone. "Your dad's on his way."

———

ANNA LAY on her bed in the darkness, clutching her small, gold cross pendant—a present from her mom on her seventh birthday. Her mom had smiled and said, "The pendant itself has no power. It's just a reminder of what Jesus did for you and that He is with you."

She stared up at the plastic glow-in-the-dark stars on the ceiling. Through her open door, she heard her dad talking to the police as he paced the hallway. She saw the cord from the phone in her parents' bedroom stretch as he walked past.

Most of his speech was muffled. But she caught snippets—something about having to wait twenty-four hours to report a missing person. Earlier, he had called all their friends and acquaintances. No one had seen her mom.

She crawled out of bed, knelt beside it, and prayed. *Dear God, please bring my mom home. Please, please, please . . .*

CHAPTER 2
THIRTY YEARS LATER

Extraordinary things often happen on ordinary days. That's a saying Anna had heard. But she never thought it would apply to her.

Anna piled her light-brown hair on the top of her head and secured it with an elastic band. She had dreamt about her mom again. This time, the dream didn't involve anything specific. It was more of a feeling, a longing to see her.

She stood on her tip-toes, leaned her slender frame toward the mirror, and squinted her warm dusky blue eyes. *Is that line on my forehead deeper?* She shrugged it off. It was time to get to work.

She loved working from home. She got to sleep later *and* wear pajama pants. Not to mention the easy commute down the hallway to her desk in the loft.

She padded down the stairs to make coffee. As she entered the kitchen, a nine-foot door in the back wall of the house caught her eye.

The door matched the others. She loved the tall, narrow four-panel doors with the bronze levers. But this door hadn't been there before.

Anna looked out the window beside it. She saw Mr. Hagestrom's house in the distance on the right, Mrs. Garwood's house on the left, and the big oak tree in the backyard. The sky looked gloomy. Although the snow had mostly melted, the dark clouds threatened to make it a winter wonderland again.

She closed the shutter and stared at the door. She wondered if she was dreaming. But it didn't *feel* like a dream.

Anna touched the door. It was smooth, and the lever was cool in her hand. She pushed down and felt the latch move.

She opened the door a few inches and saw a living room on her right. It looked like a continuation of their house. She swung the door wide and saw a large kitchen on her left. Beyond the living room and kitchen, a long hallway stretched out until it disappeared around a curve.

It didn't make sense. Her mind raced, trying to reconcile the incongruency. She closed the door and went to the refrigerator to get a bottle of water.

There were only three options. One, she was dreaming and would wake up at any moment. Two, she had lost her mind, and the door was a hallucination. Or three, the door was somehow real.

She sipped the water while contemplating the door. When she turned back, it was gone. It was like the door had never been there.

She felt the wall where the door had been. The rough texture of the paint had replaced the smoothness of the door. It had seemed so real. The door had been solid—at least, it had seemed like it was at the time. She decided not to tell anyone about the door, not even her husband, Dustin.

Anna forgot about making coffee and went upstairs to start working. Her hands shook as she typed the password to log on to her computer. It took several tries before she got it right. She didn't like the possibility that she might be losing her grip on reality.

But she soon got into the rhythm of her work. Numerous documents awaited her edits. Before long, she had forgotten about the door.

———

The following Monday, Anna stood in her closet deciding what she would wear for her virtual meeting. She took a violet button-down shirt off the hanger. Then she added a black cardigan. Her pajama pants would be fine; no one would be able to see them. At least half of her would be comfortable.

She pulled her hair back into a loose chignon like Mrs. Garwood wore. She adopted the style long ago; it was easy to do and professional-looking. Then she put on a little eyeliner and mascara and called it good.

Anna hurried down the stairs. She only had ten minutes to make breakfast before starting work.

When she opened the cabinet to get a drinking glass, she saw something from the corner of her eye: white where there should have been tan paint. Suede, to be exact. She remembered picking out the color when she and Dustin renovated her childhood home. The choice was between khaki and suede. The colors were similar, but the khaki had a yellow undertone she didn't like. So, she decided on suede.

But instead of a completely suede wall, there was white. She turned and saw the door. It was back.

She tilted her head as she gazed at it. It looked so real. She set the glass on the counter and went over to the door. It was smooth, and the lever was cool, like before.

Anna forgot about work. She opened the door and surveyed the rooms and the long hallway beyond them. What would happen if she stepped through?

She decided to do a test. After pulling the blueberries from the refrigerator and putting a few in her hand, she lobbed a single blueberry through the door. It crossed the threshold, fell to the floor, and rolled to a stop.

The blueberry seemed intact. She threw a few more. They landed in the living room and rolled to a stop.

Then she held her breath and poked her finger through the doorway. No harm came to her finger. Yet, she still wasn't sure she wanted to step through.

Last week, the door disappeared when she closed it and turned away. What if it vanished while she was inside? Would she disappear along with it? Maybe it would be okay if she left it open and didn't go too far?

She squeezed her eyes shut and extended her foot over the threshold. When she opened her eyes, she saw that nothing weird had happened. She pulled her foot back and thought about it. But she lost her nerve. She closed the door and went upstairs without her breakfast.

At 10:00, Anna clicked on the virtual meeting link. She unmuted herself and greeted her colleagues. They chatted about their weekends. But everyone went silent when the chief editor came onto the screen.

The chief had a long list of agenda items. Among other things, there was a new procedure for submitting edits and something about an upcoming change in software. Anna counted the faces: there were sixteen of them. The image of herself was so small that she wondered why she had bothered with the mascara.

She tried to pay attention, but her mind wandered to the door. Why hadn't she gone through it? What if she didn't get another chance to explore?

The sound of her name interrupted her thoughts. She looked up at the screen. The chief was trying to get her attention.

"Yes, what is it?" Anna asked.

"Your report?"

"Sorry, just a moment." She pushed away her thoughts of the door, refocused on work, and found her notes. The door would have to wait.

CHAPTER 3

Anna waited for Monday to arrive. Would the door appear like it had in the last two weeks? On Sunday, Dustin looked at her and asked what was wrong.

"Just thinking."

"Thinking about what?"

"Nothing important."

He put his hand on her arm. "The look on your face says it's important."

"I was wondering how I ended up editing instruction manuals. It's boring and unsatisfying." It was true. She had wondered about that lately, even if she hadn't been thinking about it just then. So it wasn't *technically* a lie, right?

He leaned back on the couch. "I understand. I never thought I'd end up working as a tax attorney, finding ways for rich people to keep their money." He smiled. "After all, I went to law school to seek justice for the oppressed."

Anna laughed. "Yeah, whenever you talk about your work, I get sleepy."

Dustin started reading a book, and she returned to her thoughts about the door. She hoped it would be there. She kicked herself a little for chickening out when she had the chance to go through it.

On Monday morning, Anna rushed downstairs at 7:50, hoping to see the door. It was there. Anna grinned and walked over to it.

She opened the door wide and looked at what she could see through the opening. The blueberries were gone. But the living room was still on her right, with the kitchen on her left. After fifty feet, the hallway curved and disappeared from her sight.

She extended her foot over the threshold like before and pulled it back. And then she took a step. The sound around her changed, enveloping her in silence.

Anna took a few steps, looking over her shoulder at the door. It was still open; she saw her kitchen on the other side. And then the scent of freshly baked cookies met her nose.

She walked into the kitchen. It was bigger than her own. Beautiful maple cabinets lined the walls, topped with crown molding. The island's marble countertop extended over a large area: two sides were straight, and the other two formed an arc. She saw a dozen evenly spaced stools under the counter. It looked like a picture from a home improvement magazine.

Next to the stove sat a plate of chocolate chip cookies. Intrigued, she picked one up. It was warm and soft, just how she liked them. She took a bite, and the chocolate melted in her mouth.

She finished eating it and went over to a large, built-in refrigerator. It was filled with a variety of fresh fruit and vegetables. An unopened glass milk bottle sat on the shelf. She looked back at the door. It was still open.

She pulled out the milk bottle and closed the refrigerator.

After setting it on the counter, she searched for a glass. The cabinets held a variety of dishes, along with serving bowls and platters, enough for a dinner party. When she found a glass, she poured herself some milk.

As she ate a second cookie and drank the milk, she wondered what she was doing. What if the cookies and milk weren't safe? They could be poisoned or something. Yet, it all seemed not only okay but *good*.

A window over the kitchen sink caught her eye. She peered out, but her neighbors' houses and the large oak tree were nowhere to be seen. She gasped at the sight of the rolling green hills and wildflowers. The pastoral landscape clashed with her earlier glimpse of wintertime from her bedroom window.

Where was she? Fear washed over her. She rushed back through the door, took one last look at this new, exciting place, and closed it.

She glanced at the clock in her kitchen: 8:30. How could that be? She had been gone for five, maybe seven minutes, at the most.

Anna poured herself a glass of water. She looked at the wall where the door had been. It was gone.

ANNA THOUGHT all week about the door. She wanted to tell Dustin—to share the experience with him. But she decided against it.

It wasn't so much that he wouldn't believe her. How *could* he? No evidence of the door remained. It sounded crazy. Doors didn't just appear in your kitchen and take you to alternate realities.

Instead, she waited for the next Monday to see if the door would return. She woke up at 6:30 to give herself more time to explore if it appeared. She listened for Dustin to leave for work. When she heard the garage door open and close, she jumped out of bed and raced downstairs. It was back.

Anna smiled. She felt the familiar lever and opened the door. Everything looked just like it had before. She stepped through the doorway with more confidence. The Big Kitchen was still on her left, with the window she had looked through.

She inched down the hallway to see what else she would find, pausing often to take in her surroundings. Paintings by Van Gogh, Monet, Renoir, and other impressionist painters hung on the walls. She also saw stunning landscape photographs by Fielder. They were all pictures she had admired at one time or another.

The hallway branched off into smaller hallways, leading to what appeared to be bedrooms, bathrooms, and sitting rooms. Anna even saw dining rooms and smaller kitchens. She stayed on the main hallway path so she wouldn't get lost. Every window revealed the rolling green hills she had seen the week before.

The hallway curved. As she walked around the arched pathway, one of the branches led down a smaller hallway on her left. But to her right, a foyer opened into a large oval room lined with books from floor to ceiling. Her face lit up as she turned in a circle, admiring the library's walls. She saw delicate flowers carved into the maple shelves, leather-bound volumes, and a ladder waiting for someone to ascend it to choose a title.

Anna pushed the ladder. It moved silently on its track. She stopped it and climbed the rungs midway up the wall. Now that she was close, she realized the titles weren't printed on the spines. *That's inefficient. How are you supposed to find anything?*

She pulled out a volume. *The Winter of Our Discontent*, by John Steinbeck. She put it back and chose another. *The Holy Bible*. An image of her mom's Bible flashed into her mind. She had kept it but hadn't looked at it in years.

She continued randomly selecting books. There were titles

by the Bronte sisters, John Grisham, Charles Dickens, and Joel Rosenberg. All her favorite authors were accounted for.

Anna settled on a book she hadn't read in a while and climbed down the ladder. She sank into a large recliner and relaxed. And then she smelled it—the aroma of freshly baked cookies. They were on an end table beside the chair with a glass of cold milk.

It was eerie. But Anna couldn't help but smile. Everything she wanted was right here. She reveled in the break from her dull editing job. In college, she had wanted to be a writer. But life had different plans for her.

She picked up a cookie and opened the book. It looked new, and a freshly printed scent emanated from the paper. She read, "*Sense and Sensibility*: A Novel, by Jane Austen." And on the title page, she saw an elegant handwritten note:

For Anna, Enjoy! Jane Austen

Anna's heart jumped as she gaped at the book. Was this some sort of joke? The spell was broken, and the hairs on her neck stood up. She snapped the book shut, dropped it beside the cookies and milk, and dashed into the main hallway.

As she hurried around the curve, she saw the open door in the distance. Relieved, she half ran toward the door as her steps echoed in the silence. When she reached the door, she stepped through and shut it behind her. She didn't realize her palms were sweating until her hand slid off the bronze lever.

She breathed in deeply, held it for a moment, and then exhaled slowly. She was safe; she was home.

CHAPTER 4

That evening, Anna looked through her books in the loft. She pulled her mom's Bible off the shelf and opened it. It was filled with sticky notes, highlights, and notes in the margins. As she flipped through the pages, a passage highlighted in purple caught her eye.

And we know that all things work together for good . . .

Really? All things? How could her mom's disappearance ever be good? She closed the Bible and put it away. *I didn't need God then, and I don't need Him now.* She thought the words. Yet deep in her heart, she knew they weren't true.

She refocused her thoughts on what had happened earlier in the day. She found her copy of *Sense and Sensibility* and took it downstairs to read on the couch. The tattered paperback smelled musty.

She couldn't stop thinking about the note in the book on the other side of the door. She retraced her steps and everything she had seen, trying to make sense of it. But she still couldn't bring herself to tell Dustin about it. Even she was having a hard time believing what she saw.

"Hey, Anna. Did you hear me?"

Anna looked up. She hadn't heard Dustin come upstairs from his workout in the basement. His dark brown hair was messy, and his almond-brown eyes looked annoyed as he stared at her.

"What did you say?" she asked.

"My parents want us to come over for dinner next Friday. Is that okay with you?"

"Sure. Ask them what we should bring."

Dustin left the room as he texted his mom. When he was gone, Anna went back to her thoughts. Should she go through the door if it showed up again? She felt a pull to go back. But was it safe? *Well, nothing bad has happened to me yet. On the contrary, it's filled with things I love.*

As she reasoned inside herself, Dustin came back into the room. "It's all set. Dinner's at 6:00 next Friday. We're supposed to bring dessert."

"What do you want me to make?" she asked.

"How about your cherry chocolate cake?"

"That sounds good."

Anna smiled. She had decided she would go back through the door. And this time, she would take a day off to enjoy some time away.

On Monday, Anna wasted no time. After Dustin left for work, she got out of bed, washed her face, and pulled her hair back in a ponytail. Then she grabbed her slippers and went downstairs.

The door waited for her. She pushed on the cool lever and opened it. After taking inventory of what she expected to see, she ensured the door was wide open and stepped through. She already knew what she wanted to do. Instead of exploring, she would read a book in the library, eat some cookies, and then take a nap.

She noted the living room on her right and the Big Kitchen on her left and started down the hallway. Her slippers made a shuffling sound as she walked. She hadn't noticed the extent of the silence before. She stopped. She heard the air moving through her nose as she breathed in and out. But there was no hum from any of the refrigerators. Nor did the HVAC make any noise.

She walked around the hallway's curve and turned right into the library. The end table was empty; the cookies, milk, and book were gone. She pushed the ladder to where the book had been last week. She climbed up and found it—right where it had been.

Anna listened carefully. She didn't hear anyone and was pretty sure she was alone. *If warm cookies and cold milk spontaneously show up, I guess the book can put itself away.*

She climbed down, sank into the chair, and opened the book. The handwritten note was still there. She turned the page and started to read.

Before she knew it, she smelled the cookies. Looking over, she saw the plate on the end table, with a glass of cold milk. She picked up a cookie and took a bite as she immersed herself in the story. After their father died, the three Dashwood sisters and their widowed mother had to leave their family's estate at Norland Park and move to a much smaller Barton Cottage.

Anna read about halfway through the book. Then, growing sleepy, she decided it was time for a quick nap. She noted the page she was on and placed the volume on the end table. Then, she walked across the main hallway and down a smaller hallway until she found a bedroom.

Crisp linens and a quilt with subtle floral patterns covered a cherry wood four-poster bed. The quilt was her favorite color: lavender. Pillows lined the headboard, and soft light filtered through a skylight.

She looked in the closet. Besides wooden hangers, it was empty. No clothes hung from the rod.

Anna pulled down the quilt. As she lay down, a brief impression that a nap wasn't a good idea passed through her mind. But it was quickly replaced by the thought of how soft, yet firm, the pillow was. It was just perfect. And then she was fast asleep.

***

As Anna surfaced from a dream state, she looked around her. Nothing seemed familiar at first. It was like she had awoken from a dream inside a dream. When she fully regained consciousness, she remembered. She pushed down the lavender quilt and wondered how long she had been there.

It was disconcerting not knowing the time. It never seemed to get dark. And she hadn't seen any clocks.

She hurried up the main hallway. As she rounded the curve, she saw the open door. Rushing past the Big Kitchen, she went through the door and shut it behind her. Then she looked at the clock. It was 4:30. And it was light outside.

She let out a huge breath. Relieved she hadn't been gone too long, she turned her thoughts to making dinner before Dustin got home. She examined the refrigerator's contents. Then she opened the freezer. She took out a package of ground beef and started thawing it in the microwave.

As she opened the large drawer under the stove to take out a skillet, she jumped at the sound of Dustin's voice.

"Where have you been?"

She looked up from the drawer and placed her hand over her chest. "Oh, wow, you startled me. Why aren't you at work?"

"I've been looking all over for you." His gruff voice

matched the thin line of his lips. "And the police have been looking too."

Anna met her husband's gaze. There were dark circles under his eyes, and his hair was disheveled. He looked like he hadn't been sleeping. How long had she been gone?

"What day is it?" Anna asked.

He wrinkled his brow. "It's Friday."

Friday? Her stomach churned. Four days? How could she have been gone that long? She thought she had only lain down for a few minutes. Anna looked at the floor. She didn't know what to say.

"Where are your shoes and coat? You didn't go out in your pajamas, did you? It's freezing out there."

"I didn't go outside."

"I know you were outside," Dustin said. "I heard the door close when you came in."

Anna stared at her feet.

"Where did you sleep the last four nights?"

Anna felt like a deer caught in the headlights of an oncoming car.

"Stop fiddling with your cross pendant and answer me."

Anna knew she had to tell him. But how? The door was gone. And he must not have seen it while she was on the other side. Hadn't it been open the entire time she was away? It didn't make sense. If she told him, he would think she was crazy.

She doubted he'd believe her, but she didn't feel like she had a choice. "Can we sit down?"

CHAPTER 5

Anna relayed her adventures over the last few weeks. As she did, she watched Dustin's face grow even more troubled. She explained how the door appeared only on Monday mornings, how she left it open when she went through, how she planned on lying down for just a few minutes, how she fell asleep, and how time seemed to work differently between here and there.

Dustin rubbed the back of his neck while he looked at the table. Then he shook his head. "No, really, where have you been? You've been gone for *four* days."

"I already told you. I—"

"That doesn't make any sense."

"I know you think I'm making it up. But it's true." She didn't know what else to say.

"I want to believe you. But really, Anna? A magical door in our kitchen? You can't be serious."

"I know how it sounds." She paused. What if the door came back? Then she could show him. "I know you think I'm lying—or crazy—or both. But what if we took a vacation day from work on Monday? I'll show you where I've been."

Dustin grimaced. "Your work. I forgot to call them."

"That's alright," Anna said. "I'll deal with that." Work felt like the least of her worries.

He got up and started pacing. Her eyes followed him, waiting for the verdict.

"Okay," he said. "Do I have a choice?" Dustin jumped as his phone buzzed in his pocket. He looked at it and frowned. "It's my dad. I completely forgot about dinner tonight. I need to let him know we're not coming."

"You didn't tell them I was missing?"

"I didn't need the added stress of dealing with them." Dustin walked toward the den as he answered the call. "Hi, Dad. I'm sorry. We completely forgot about dinner."

She listened as his voice trailed off. At least she wouldn't have to try to explain anything to them.

LATER THAT EVENING, Anna checked the messages on her phone. There weren't any. She logged on to her work laptop. She saw an email about a meeting next Thursday and a few messages from one of her colleagues.

Other than that, it looked like she hadn't been missed. Her work was solitary. Besides a few meetings each month, she didn't interact with anyone that much.

She emailed the chief editor, letting her know she would be taking Monday off. She also responded to her coworker's messages, apologizing for not seeing them earlier. She gave the excuse of not getting the notification—something that happened frequently.

She resolved to work on Saturday and Sunday to catch up on some of the work she had missed. Then she closed the laptop and went to bed.

Dustin turned on his side. In the moonlight, he could see the outline of Anna's frame in the bed. He tried to quiet his mind, but sleep eluded him.

He was grateful she was home—that she was physically safe. But her outlandish story didn't make sense. There hadn't been an open doorway in the kitchen while she was gone. All he saw was a wall.

Why couldn't she tell him the truth? Maybe she'd had an affair and couldn't own up to it. Yet, that didn't seem to fit either. She had still been in the pajamas he saw her wearing on Sunday night when they went to bed. It all felt so weird.

He sighed. He'd give her until Monday morning like she asked, and then they'd talk. It was going to be a long weekend.

As Anna showered on Monday, she wondered if Dustin thought she had lost her mind. If the door didn't show up, this day would go poorly.

At 7:30, they went downstairs. There was no door yet. But she wasn't ready to give up hope.

They decided to eat breakfast while they waited. Anna picked at her English muffin. Normally, she would have savored the apricot jam, but her stomach felt queasy. The door was now more about proving her sanity than adventure.

"It's almost 8:00," Dustin said. "How much longer are we going to wait?"

"Give it a little more—" As she looked up to plead with him, she saw the door. "Wait, there it is."

"There's what?"

"The door." Anna's excitement waned, and fear took its place. Was she crazy after all? She walked to the door, reached out, and held the cool, bronze lever. "You can't see it?"

"No."

Anna opened the door and looked at the now-familiar

rooms and hallway. As she stepped into the doorway, Dustin said, "Wait! Where did you—?"

She heard him cry out, but his speech cut off mid-sentence. Anna stepped back into their kitchen. "Did you see me go through it?"

"That was bizarre. You were there, and then you weren't."

She reached out. "Here, take my hand." When Dustin took hold of it, she stepped into the doorway again.

Dustin couldn't believe his eyes. He watched as Anna disappeared into the wall. Only her hand was left, pulling on his. The sound of her voice had vanished with her body.

He resisted for a moment. Then he closed his eyes and followed the tug of her hand.

"Are you okay?" Anna asked.

The sound of the space was different. It had a calm, peaceful vibe. He opened his eyes and saw Anna grinning at him.

"Strange, isn't it?" she said.

Anna pointed out the living room, the Big Kitchen, and the hallway. It looked just as she had described it. When he turned around, he saw an open doorway with their kitchen beyond. It was surreal. He resisted the urge to run back through the door.

"Wow, you weren't lying, were you?" Dustin said.

"Isn't it amazing?"

Anna started by showing Dustin the Big Kitchen. A plate of chocolate chip cookies and two glasses of cold milk welcomed them. "The cookies are delicious. Try one."

"Where did they come from?"

"I don't know. They always appear out of nowhere."

"Yeah, but how? Someone has to bake them, right?"

"Like I said, I don't know. Remember when I told you how they just appeared while I was reading a book in the library?"

"Yeah."

"No one brought them. I would have seen or heard them if they had. One moment, the cookies weren't there, and the next moment, they were."

Dustin creased his brow. "How do we know they're safe? They could be poisoned."

"I've eaten them before, and nothing bad happened to me." Anna picked up a cookie and handed it to Dustin. It was warm and soft like before.

She grabbed one for herself and took a bite. "See? I didn't keel over and die. Try it." Anna took another bite and closed her eyes as the chocolate melted in her mouth.

"Mmmm . . . this *is* good."

Dustin's comment echoed her thoughts. She drank the milk. Dustin dunked his cookie.

"I could get used to this," Dustin said.

"I want to show you everything I've seen so far," Anna said.

"Okay. Have you ever seen anyone?"

"No." Had she seen anyone? Except for a brief moment, she hadn't really considered it. She didn't like the idea of someone living in her mysterious getaway.

"I saw fresh fruit and veggies in the fridge. But I haven't seen any evidence of anyone being here—no dust, crumbs, trash, or dishes in the sink. Nothing. And everything looks brand new. It's like it was prepared for someone who never showed up."

"Well, we should keep an eye out."

Anna nodded. "Are you ready?"

She led him down the hallway and around the curve, pointing out the other hallways that branched off the main one. She showed him the library, the book with the hand-written note, and the chair where she had read. They gazed out the windows at the rolling green hills covered with prim-rose, snowdrops, and sweet violets.

Then they walked down the hallway to the bedroom where she had napped.

"Did you make the bed?"

"No." The bed looked untouched—its fresh, crisp sheets neatly tucked in.

"So someone else *has* been here."

"Or *something*."

"Maybe we should go back," Dustin said.

Anna agreed. Her stomach had started doing that flip-floppy thing again. How did the bed get made? There must be someone here, somewhere.

CHAPTER 6

As they stepped back through the door, Anna looked at the clock on the microwave. "Hey, Dusty. Look at the clock."

"2:35?" he said. "How can that be? We were only gone for about an hour."

"Time seems to pass differently there."

"Yeah, but it's been more than six hours. Six *hours*."

"Maybe that explains why I was gone for four days."

Dustin nodded. "If we go back, we'll have to be more careful. Next time, I'm taking my watch."

Anna smiled at Dustin. "So, you want to go back again?"

"Yeah, who wouldn't?" He pulled her close and held her in his arms. "I can't tell you how relieved I am," he said. "This past week has been incredibly difficult."

Anna lay her head on his chest, listening to his heartbeat and absorbing the moment. She loved the feeling of his strong embrace. Relieved was an understatement.

A week later, Dustin and Anna got up early and prepared for another trip through the door. Dustin put on his watch, and they went downstairs. They made breakfast sandwiches and ate in silence.

As they cleaned up their dishes, he saw Anna look up.

"The door's back," she said. "Are you ready?"

"As ready as I'll ever be." Dustin looked at his watch. "It's 8:05. I'll keep an eye on the time."

"Here, hold my hand."

Anna opened the door and stepped through. Dustin watched as Anna's body partially disappeared. He decided to close his eyes again and follow the pull of her hand. He stepped forward and heard the sound of the space change.

He opened his eyes and looked at his watch. "It's still 8:05."

"What do you want to do?" Anna asked.

"Let's take the first hallway that branches off the larger one. We can stay on it so we'll remember how to get back."

They walked past the Big Kitchen and turned left down the first smaller hallway. The hallway curved like an *S*. There were multiple bedrooms and a den furnished with a desk, office chairs, and bookshelves.

Anna looked in one of the bedrooms. It was more like a suite. It had a small sitting room with big, comfy-looking chairs and an attached bathroom with a clawfoot tub and a walk-in shower. The large white and gray marble tiles gave it a spa-like feel. It had a two-sink vanity. But there was no mirror.

"Why isn't there a mirror?" Anna asked.

"Maybe it's not finished yet."

"It looks finished to me."

"Yeah, it does. But who doesn't put a mirror in a bathroom?"

They continued walking down the hallway. After passing by multiple "suites," she still couldn't see an end.

Dustin's stomach growled.

Anna laughed. "What was that?"

"That," Dustin said, "was my stomach." He turned and grinned at Anna. "I'm hungry—in case you hadn't heard."

"Maybe we'll find a kitchen . . ." Anna's voice trailed off. A small dining room ahead had a table set for two, and the aroma of pasta sauce and warm bread filled the air.

Amidst the dishes on the table were name cards. One had "Anna" written in a fancy font, and the other read "Dustin." A large portion of lasagna, with a side salad and a bottle of vinaigrette dressing, waited on Dustin's side. On Anna's was a single-serving casserole dish with baked rigatoni. Alongside it sat a bowl of freshly grated Parmesan cheese. Between the two place settings was a basket of breadsticks.

Anna smiled and sat. But when she glanced up, Dustin stood with his arms crossed, shaking his head.

"What's wrong?" she asked.

"I don't know about this."

"You're hungry, aren't you? The meals look and smell delicious."

"They do. But something feels off."

"Can't you just enjoy it? We ate the cookies, and they were fine. We didn't get sick or anything."

"That isn't what's bothering me. How did whoever or whatever *know* I was thinking about lasagna?"

"Yeah, you're right. I was thinking about baked rigatoni." Anna paused. "Every time I've been here, this place seems to provide what I want. Maybe we should enjoy it now and talk about it later."

Dustin sat. "I guess." He took a bite of his lasagna, and his trepidation dissipated. "This is so good. You have to try it."

"Mine too."

They relaxed in their chairs and savored the food. Finished and full, they discussed what to do next.

"Should we clean up the dishes?" Dustin asked. "There's a kitchen through the doorway there."

They carried their plates into the kitchen.

"I don't see a dishwasher," Anna said.

"Let's put them in the sink," he said. "We can wash them by hand."

They searched the cabinets for dishwashing soap. Finding none, they turned back toward the sink.

"The dishes are gone," Anna said.

Dustin looked at his watch and frowned.

"What's wrong?"

"It still says it's 8:05." He pulled his cell phone out of his back pocket. "My phone also says 8:05. Let's go back. *Now.*"

He grabbed Anna's hand and beelined it toward the small hallway they had walked down. They followed it back to the main hallway, passed by the Big Kitchen, and went through the open door.

As they entered the kitchen, Dustin looked at his watch again. What? He looked up and saw it was dark outside. "Anna, it's 7:30."

"We've been gone for almost twelve hours?"

"Yeah, it doesn't make sense. Look, my watch changed when we came back through the door." He looked at the clock on the microwave. Then he pulled out his phone and compared it to his watch. They were the same.

"Where's your phone?" Dustin asked.

"On the counter."

"Since we didn't take it with us, let's check the date on it to see if it's still Monday."

Anna unlocked her phone. "Yep, it's still Monday. That's a relief."

———

THE NEXT MORNING, Anna stared at her computer screen. She had read the same sentence three times. But she still had no idea what it said. Her mind kept wandering back to the door.

How could they keep track of the time there? *Could* they keep track of it? She knew she wanted to go back. But Dustin didn't seem so sure. What if he refused?

So many questions were unanswered. She would have to wait until tonight when Dustin got home from work.

———

AFTER ANNA and Dustin cleaned up the dinner dishes, they sat at the table to talk.

"I don't think we should go back," Dustin said.

"Why not? I want to."

"It's not safe. Time works differently there. And it's unnatural. It seems to *know* things about us. I don't like the feeling I get from it."

"But it's been so much fun. I've enjoyed it every time I go."

"Something's not right."

"Nothing bad has happened to us—other than losing a little time. It's been like an adventure. Don't you want to find out what else is there?"

"I agree it was fun," Dustin said. "But what if it doesn't stay that way?"

Anna sulked. They were at an impasse. She didn't sense the overall danger like he did. "Maybe we should talk about it later."

CHAPTER 7

Anna thought about their conversation all week. On Friday, she decided to visit Mrs. Garwood and get her advice. She pulled on her coat and boots and trekked next door through the snow.

She rang the bell and watched as Mrs. Garwood opened the door. She looked like the grandmother she never had. "Hi, Mrs. Garwood. I brought you some corn chowder. I know how much you like it."

"Please, Anna, call me Lydia. Mrs. Garwood sounds so formal." She took the small crock from Anna. "Thanks for thinking of me, dear. Your corn chowder is delicious."

"Who's this?" Anna stooped to greet a black kitten with white feet and a white diamond on his chest.

"That's Max. It was time. Simon—you remember Simon, don't you?"

"Oh yes, I remember Simon."

"My dear kitty, Simon. He lived to be the ripe old age of twenty-two. They're not supposed to live that long, you know. But he's been gone so long, and I needed some company."

Anna picked up Max and rubbed his ears as she followed Mrs. Garwood into the kitchen. "He sure is cute."

"He hasn't outgrown his kitten crazies yet. But he's a keeper."

Max jumped out of Anna's arms, attacking a small mouse toy on the floor.

"Please, sit down. What's troubling you? I know that look of yours."

"How did you resolve disputes with Mr. Garwood—"

"Please, Anna. You can call him by his first name, Will."

"How did you and Will come to some sort of resolution when you argued about something?"

"What's going on with you and Dustin?"

"We had a disagreement. I want to go back to a place we've gone to before. He says it's dangerous. But I don't think it is."

"Do you think he's saying no to be mean?"

"I think he's worried about going back."

"Is there a reason he thinks it's dangerous?"

"I guess so."

"Do you agree it's a reasonable reason, even if you disagree about how dangerous it may be?"

Anna looked down. How did Mrs. Garwood always get right to the heart of it?

"You should trust your husband," Mrs. Garwood said. "He only wants to protect you."

ANNA DECIDED TO FOLLOW MRS. Garwood's advice. She even told Dustin as much. Yet, when she came downstairs and saw the door, her resolution dissolved.

She stood there, holding the cool, bronze lever. It couldn't hurt to explore a little, could it? Before she knew it, she pushed down on the lever, and the door opened. She didn't have to tell anyone. It would be her little secret.

She stepped through the door, walked past the Big Kitchen, and followed the main hallway. She walked around the curve and past the library. Today, she would look for something new.

As she walked, she saw the rolling green hills covered with flowers out of the windows. The hallway led to more bedrooms and a kitchenette with a small breakfast table. On one side of the table was a bench, and chairs were pushed in on the opposite side.

The hallway wound around the kitchenette. As she went through the bend, she saw a room enclosed with glass walls. She drew closer and saw a swimming pool. A swim sounded like fun.

Blush-rose granite tiles spanned the room, intermingled with beautiful floral mosaics in complementary tones. Lounge chairs surrounded the pool, with rolled-up beach towels waiting for someone to use them. In the corner of the room, water swirled and foamed in a hot tub.

On the back wall were two doorways. She walked through one of them into a large bathroom covered with marble tiles. Beside the bathroom was a smaller room with a bench and bronze hooks for hanging clothes. On one of the hooks hung a one-piece swimsuit.

Anna smiled. She hung up her clothes and put on the suit. Then she went back into the pool room and dipped her toes in the water. It was warm. She jumped in, swam down, touched the bottom, and surfaced. Then, she floated on her back, staring at the ceiling.

It was calming. She thought about Dustin and their life together. They had met in college—he was a senior and she a junior at the University of Denver. After he graduated, he was accepted into law school at Yale and DU. But he stayed at DU, so they wouldn't have to be apart.

They married soon after. When she got her degree in English literature, she wanted to start writing. But she went to work at a small publisher as an assistant editor and never seemed to have the time to start.

She closed her eyes. This place was amazing. She hoped Dustin would change his mind so they could share it.

When she got out of the pool, she shivered. The hot tub looked inviting. She eased her body into the water. The well-positioned jets massaged her back.

And then she smelled a familiar aroma: cookies. She looked over at a small table beside the hot tub, and there they were. Could life get any better?

Anna dried off and changed back into her clothes. She wasn't sure how long she had been there and was nervous about the time. She ran back down the hallway, around its twists and curves, by the Big Kitchen, and through the door.

Dustin sat at the table, looking at her. She closed the door and glanced at the clock on the microwave: 8:30. *Oops*. She sat at the table.

"Why is your hair wet?"

"I found a swimming pool."

They stared at each other. She couldn't tell if Dustin was mad or not.

She broke the silence. "I'm sorry. I couldn't help myself. I came downstairs this morning, and the door was there. It was like I was spellbound."

The tension was thick. What was that expression: It felt like you could cut it with a knife? "Please say something," she said.

"I was worried, Anna. I didn't know how long you'd be gone. And I couldn't look for you because I couldn't see the door. I felt the wall where the door should've been, but all I felt was a wall."

"I'm sorry. I thought I'd be back before you got home. I didn't want you to worry."

"I don't want to lose you."

She touched his arm, and he took her hand.

"Please don't go there alone anymore," he said.

"Don't go there *alone*? Does that mean you'll go with me again?"

"Yes, I'll go."

"Do you want to go to the pool?" Anna asked. "There's a hot tub and a changing room with swimming suits."

"That sounds like fun. It'll be a little summer getaway from all the snow at home."

"I can't believe it snowed two feet last night and took out our internet connection." Anna grinned. "I love a good snow day." She was excited to explore again with Dustin.

He followed her down the main hallway, past the library, and into the glass-enclosed room. There was no trace of her last visit.

She pointed to the doorways at the back of the room. "Those are the changing rooms. See you in a minute."

When Anna came out, Dustin was already in the pool. She jumped in right beside him, splashing him with water.

"Okay, game on," he said.

They played water volleyball, swam, and floated until their fingers were like prunes. Then they relaxed in the hot tub.

"It's been a great day," he said. "But you know what would make it even better? Some cheeseburgers, fries, and a shake."

Anna looked over at the table beside the hot tub. "Well, there you go. It just got better."

Two plates with burgers and fries sat there waiting for them, along with a strawberry shake and a peanut butter chocolate one.

"I think this is the first time I'm not weirded out that food just shows up out of nowhere." Dustin plucked a fry off the plate. "Let's sit over there and eat."

They wrapped themselves in towels and took the plates to a small table with chairs.

"This is much nicer than trying to keep warm by the fire at home," Anna said. "I think something's wrong with that old heater."

"Yeah, we might need to replace it soon. But for now, we have the hot tub."

Anna smiled. "I'm glad you came back with me again."

"Me too."

CHAPTER 8

Mondays off became a regular thing. Sometimes, they took a vacation day from work. Other times, they worked on a Saturday instead.

Soon, Anna and Dustin grew used to exploring on the other side of the door. They spent an entire day walking down the main hallway to see how far it would go. But they never saw an end to it. They spent other days choosing one of the smaller hallways that branched off the main one. It was always the same. No matter how far they walked, it just kept going.

After a while, they noticed certain things were always the same. For one, a soft light continually filtered through the windows. The sun never set. The wildflowers on the rolling green hills didn't fade. And they never saw a clock, a mirror, or a TV.

They grew adept at *feeling* how long they had been there. So far, they returned by Monday night without fail. Of course, that limited their ability to explore the vastness of wherever the place was.

Then one evening, Anna asked Dustin, "What if we stayed more than a day?"

"More than a day?" Dustin shook his head. "I don't know if that would be a good idea."

"We could take a few days off from work. Then we'd be able to go farther down the main hallway. Maybe we could find a door that leads outside?"

"I'm running out of vacation time."

"So am I. Maybe just once?"

"I'll look at my work schedule tomorrow."

Anna's eyes twinkled. The promise of adventure never grew old.

"Hi, Anna dear." Mrs. Garwood smiled warmly. "Come on in. I'm so glad you visit like your mother did."

"I brought you some brownies."

Mrs. Garwood hugged Anna. "They look absolutely scrumptious. Set them on the table and have a seat."

"I brought your laptop too," Anna said. "I set it up so it'll automatically connect to Wi-Fi here and at our house."

"Thank you so much, dear. What would I do without you?"

Anna set the brownies down and slid the backpack off her shoulder. She put the backpack on a chair, pulled the slim laptop out of its protective covering, and placed it on the table.

"Would you like some tea?" Mrs. Garwood asked.

"Sure, that would be great." Anna watched as Mrs. Garwood took two porcelain tea cups from the cupboard. She boiled water in an electric kettle and poured it into a teapot that matched the cups. Then she set the tea service on the table and sat.

"I don't know why, but I've been thinking about my mom a lot lately." Anna stirred three lumps of sugar into her tea.

"She was a lovely woman. I enjoyed getting lost in our conversations during our afternoons together."

Anna sipped her tea and looked at her lap. Her eyes were watery, and she didn't want Mrs. Garwood to see.

"You know," Mrs. Garwood said, "it's natural to go through seasons of thinking about a loved one who's no longer with you."

Max jumped into Mrs. Garwood's lap and nudged her hand with his head.

"I think about my Will every day at some point. But there are times I can't get him off my mind."

Anna nodded. "That makes sense. I wish I knew what happened to her."

"So do I. It's difficult not knowing. I'm sorry you had to go through all of that." Mrs. Garwood reached over and squeezed her hand.

Anna changed the subject. "We might be going on vacation soon."

"Where are you going?"

"I'm not sure yet. We're looking at our schedules to see when we can get away. Then we'll plan." Anna didn't know why she started talking about vacation. She didn't want to even hint at the door. "Are you thinking of going anywhere?"

"Oh, no. I'm fine right here. Max and I are just fine."

***

A few weeks later, Anna stood by the door with Dustin beside her. "Are you ready?" she asked.

"Let's go."

Anna pushed on the cool, bronze lever, opened the door, and took Dustin's hand. She took a step, and they walked through the door together. Anna looked back, made sure the door was wide open, and started down the main hallway.

They had three days to discover where the main hallway

led. Dustin had taken off two weeks from work—just in case they were gone longer than they intended. He thought she had also taken time off. But she had quit her job and hadn't told him yet.

Now that they were familiar with much of their surroundings, they hurried past the Big Kitchen, around the curve, past the library, through the twists and turns of the hallway, past the pool, and beyond. When they reached the farthest point of their previous journey, they took a short break. Lunch was waiting for them in a small dining room. They ate their sandwiches and got back on the path.

"I don't think I'll ever get used to the food showing up out of nowhere," Dustin said. "It's still so bizarre."

"Me either."

"Let's try to keep a faster pace, so maybe we'll be able to reach the end."

They continued walking down the hallway. It went on and on, curving past more bedrooms, suites, sitting rooms, kitchens, and dining rooms. Like before, they gazed at the rolling green hills and wildflowers as they passed each window.

"I'm getting tired," Anna said. "Can we take another break?" She slumped down in a big, comfy chair and looked up at Dustin.

"Of course." He sat in the chair beside her. "We have a little longer before we'll have to head back."

"What's that?" Anna asked.

"What's what?"

"Look over there." Anna pointed. "It looks like a guitar."

She got up, walked toward a smaller hallway that branched off the main one, and stopped in front of a doorway. "It *is* a guitar."

Dustin followed her. As she walked through the doorway, Anna saw Martin, Gibson, and Taylor guitars hanging from the walls. In the far corner, there was a Bösendorfer piano with its bench pulled out ever so slightly.

She picked up a guitar and strummed it. It sounded like it was in tune. Then she went to the piano and sat.

"Will you play something for me?" she asked.

"I don't know. It's been a long time."

"Please?"

Dustin sat next to her at the piano. Before long, the eighteenth variation of Rachmaninoff's Rhapsody on a Theme of Paganini filled the room. Anna lost herself in the beautiful, haunting music.

When he finished, Anna looked at him. "Why don't we have a piano? You play so well. I love hearing it."

"There's no room for a piano."

"We can make room."

"We can't afford a piano."

"Well, maybe not a Bösendorfer. But we could still get a decent one."

Dustin's face had lost the calm enjoyment it wore while he was playing. "Let's keep going before we run out of time," he said.

They continued at a brisk pace down the main hallway. There were more twists and turns and an assortment of regular rooms. Yet, there was no sign of the hallway coming to an end. Nor were there any doorways leading outside.

After a while, Dustin stopped. "We should head back. It's been about one and a half days in real time."

Anna nodded. They turned around and started the long trek toward their house. Soon, they passed the music room. She was already tired of walking. It somehow seemed longer on their way back. But after a while, they reached the swimming pool and then the library.

As they went around the final curve and past the Big Kitchen, Anna looked up. Instead of an open doorway with their kitchen on the other side, there was a wall.

"Where's the door?" he asked.

"It should be right here, to the left of the Big Kitchen. But I don't see it." She walked to where the door should have been and touched the wall. Her stomach felt like it was tied in knots. What if they couldn't go back?

"Did you close the door?" he asked.

"No."

"Then how did it close?"

"I don't know."

"Well, it didn't just close itself."

"Didn't it?"

Anna twisted her hands. The whole thing was still mysterious to her. But one thing she was certain of was the location of the door. And it was gone.

CHAPTER 9
MARY

Few would blame Mary for the decision she was about to make. In her shoes, they would likely do the same.

As she walked up the small hallway toward the Big Kitchen, she cursed the day she found the door. It had been something new and enticing on a mundane day—an escape from the drudgery of laundry, cooking, and cleaning. She should have known there would be consequences.

At first, it seemed like a dream come true. After all, it was beautiful here. And peaceful. But the dream turned to horror when the choice to be there was taken from her.

Now, the quiet was a constant reminder of what she had lost. Family. Friends. Simple things like talking to someone, the feel of her husband's embrace, or holding her child's hand.

She didn't know how long she had been there. Marking the passage of time was difficult. The sun never set. There was always fresh food. And nothing ever seemed to wear out. After you used something and walked away, it returned to its former, unused condition. She didn't know *how*. But it did, every time.

Mary was lost in her thoughts when the silence was broken. It sounded like someone talking. At first, she thought she was hearing things. But the volume of their voices increased as she moved closer to the Big Kitchen.

Then she saw them—a man and a woman walking down the main hallway. Where did they come from? She hadn't seen anyone since she had come here.

She hid behind a large, leather-upholstered recliner and watched as they walked away from her toward the library. She couldn't quite make out what they were talking about. The man must have said something funny because the woman laughed and pushed on his arm.

When they were gone, she went into the Big Kitchen. Her eyes grew wide when she saw the open door. She couldn't believe it. It was in the same place where she had come into this place on that fateful day long ago.

Mary looked through it and saw a smaller kitchen on the other side. It didn't look like her kitchen. Still, it was somewhere other than here.

She hesitated, contemplating whether she should go through the door. She didn't know where that kitchen was or what she would encounter. But it couldn't be worse than here, could it?

She took a deep breath, stepped through the door, and closed it behind her.

MARY SMILED TO HERSELF. She had finally escaped that place. She glanced behind her; the door had vanished.

And then a wave of anxiety washed over her. Why had she closed the door? Why didn't she leave it open so the man and the woman could come back? She felt uneasy, but she pushed away the thoughts. She had to figure out where she was.

Mary looked around her. Though smaller, the kitchen was beautiful. The earthen tones of the cabinets, granite countertops, and wood flooring complemented each other.

She stood still, taking in her new surroundings and listening intently for any sounds. A train whistled in the distance. A clock ticked away the seconds. The refrigerator hummed. Otherwise, it was quiet. She didn't think anyone else was there. But the only way she could be certain was to look.

She opened the door beside the kitchen and saw a garage. Two cars were parked inside. Then she walked down the hallway. Leather couches lined the living room, and a large, mirror-like thing hung on the wall. There was also a small bathroom, a formal dining room, and a den on her left.

She jumped as the chimes of a grandfather clock echoed through the silence. It was 11:00—wherever she was.

At the end of the hallway was a door. It looked like a regular door. She peered out of the window beside it at the snow-covered lawn. Large, fluffy snowflakes fell from the dark sky. The winter landscape sharply contrasted with the rolling green hills she had become accustomed to seeing.

To the right of the door, a staircase led to the second floor. She climbed the stairs, taking one step at a time and stopping to listen. At the top, a small hallway split in two directions, each with doorways leading into other rooms. She went left and walked into what appeared to be the master bedroom.

The large bedroom had a vaulted, tray ceiling lined with crown moulding. Soft, earthen tones that matched the kitchen covered the walls. A king-sized canopy bed with simple, modern lines looked inviting with its chambray-colored quilt and matching pillow shams.

Doorways opened into a walk-in closet and a bathroom. She looked in the closet; there were men's and women's clothes inside. Two toothbrushes were in the holder on the sink.

After going through the upstairs, it looked like only two people lived there. And two people had gone through the door. She was alone. Only the master bedroom was lived in: two bedrooms were empty, and a third had boxes stacked in it.

The end of the hallway opened into a loft overlooking the stairs with a desk and bookcases.

Mary went downstairs. Stopping at the front door, she worked up her courage. She longed to feel fresh air on her face.

On the other side of the door, she had never gone outside. Not once. She had looked for a door so she could stroll in the beautiful countryside. But she had never found one. Not only was it doorless, but none of the windows opened. She often imagined how it would feel, smell, and sound outside.

As she pushed the bronze lever, the door opened. A biting, cold wind rushed through it, blowing in the snow. It looked like a blizzard. She closed the door and locked it.

Mary went back to the kitchen and looked in the refrigerator. She found some lunch meat and cheese and set them on the counter. Then she searched for bread. After she made herself a sandwich, she sat at the kitchen table, trying to figure out what to do. Although she was hungry, the sandwich wasn't sitting well in her stomach.

She stared at the wall where she had come through the door, and the questions returned. Why had she closed it? Why hadn't she talked to the man and woman instead of hiding? *You're a coward.*

Exhausted, she put her plate in the sink and decided it was time for a nap. She felt uncomfortable as she set up a makeshift bed on the couch. It didn't feel right to sleep in their bed. So she used the blankets and throw pillows on the sofa.

Mary lay on the couch and pulled the blanket up to her chin. The wind whistled and howled, and the crystallized snow pelted against the windowpane.

She looked around the room. Shadows clung to the walls. *It must be the storm making it so dark.* A fireplace mantel was covered with picture frames, and the mirror-like thing hung on the wall across from her.

Her eyes were heavy. The grandfather clock chimed twice, and she fell into a deep sleep.

"Mommy?"

Mary felt hands, arms, and legs as a tiny frame climbed over her and onto the bed.

"Mommy?"

"Ssshhh, JoJo," Mary whispered. "Daddy's sleeping."

"I had a bad dream," JoJo said.

Mary pulled JoJo close and felt little arms wrap around her neck. "What was it?"

"You were gone, and I couldn't find you." JoJo's small voice wavered.

"It's okay, JoJo. I'm not going anywhere." Mary held JoJo. "Do you want to sleep with me and Daddy?"

JoJo nodded, and Mary felt Jim's arm wrap around them.

MARY SHIVERED. She reached for JoJo but felt empty space and cold leather. The chimes of a grandfather clock grew louder as she regained consciousness. And then she remembered: she had escaped from that place.

She fought to hold on to her dream with JoJo in her arms and the warmth of Jim's embrace. But it was slipping away. She felt tears welling up in her eyes and forced them back. Now was not the time for a pity party.

Her stomach grumbled. She got up and looked at the clock. It was 10:00. As she peeked through one of the shutters, she saw a world of white. Small whirlwinds of snow blew over the landscape, making it difficult to distinguish anything. But it was light enough to see. How had she slept so long?

Mary walked into the kitchen and opened the refrigerator.

On the top shelf, she saw strawberries and strawberry yogurt. That sounded good. She took them from the fridge and set them on the counter.

Looking through the cabinets, she found a bowl and a drawer with utensils. She washed a few strawberries, cut them into slices, and put them in the bowl. Then she added the yogurt and mixed them together.

Mary ate her breakfast at the kitchen table, staring at the wall. She thought about the man and woman again. What would be their fate now? She scolded herself for closing the door.

Her dream nagged at her. Where were JoJo and Jim? Were they looking for her? How could she find them?

She missed everything about them—even the things that had irritated her. Why was she so annoyed when Jim left his socks on the bedroom floor? Or when JoJo interrupted her for the umpteenth time while she was reading a book? Those things seemed trivial now. She would give anything to be with them.

And how long had she been gone? She had attempted to keep track of the time. Yet, it had been difficult with the perpetual daylight and springtime.

She knew she had been gone a long time. But surely it hadn't been more than a year. And then it struck her—her hair had been cut in a short bob when she left. It had been chin-length, a little longer in the front so it would taper toward her face. And now it hung below her waist.

If she could measure it, maybe that would tell her how long she'd been away. Hair grew about half an inch a month. She got up to look for a sewing tape measure.

After rummaging through several drawers, she found what she was looking for. She held it at the nape of her neck and let it unfurl to the ground. Then she pinched it with her fingers where the tape measure met the end of her hair.

Pulling it around, she looked: it had grown about thirty

inches. *Hmmm.* Thirty times two equaled sixty months. Then sixty months divided by twelve—she had been gone for about five years.

Five years? That meant she would be thirty-six now. And JoJo would be twelve. Precious years had passed—years she would never get back.

Mary put her bowl in the sink and went into the bathroom. She stared at herself in the mirror for the first time since she had gone through the door. There hadn't been mirrors on the other side.

She couldn't believe how long her hair had grown. Her light brown locks cascaded down her back. It was unruly and in need of at least a trim. Five years? She couldn't believe she had been gone that long.

Still feeling exhausted, she went back to the couch and lay down. She stared at the ceiling and soon fell asleep.

CHAPTER 10

"Help!" Anna pounded on the wall.

"I don't think that'll do any good," Dustin said.

"It can't hurt to try."

"I couldn't hear you when you stepped through the door *while* it was open. So, I doubt anyone can hear you now."

"Good point." She sighed and turned toward Dustin.

"Are you sure you opened the door all the way?" Dustin asked.

Anna frowned. She didn't like his accusatory tone. "Yes, I'm sure. I always push it open until it touches the wall in our kitchen."

"Then, why didn't it stay open this time?"

"I don't know," she said.

"I told you it was dangerous. We never should've come in the first place."

"Stop blaming me. You came of your own free will."

She plopped down on a couch. It wasn't her fault the door closed. He was being such a jerk. She heard Dustin walking toward her, looked up, and glared at him.

"Really, Anna? Why do you have to take it so personally?" He sat on a stool in the Big Kitchen.

She crossed her arms and stared at the wall. A painting of Monet's *The Road to Chailly* hung next to where the door should have been. She hadn't noticed it before. Other times, her focus had been on the doorway with the view of their kitchen on the other side.

The picture captivated her. The road seemed to invite you to stroll down it to find out where it would lead. She could imagine herself on the path by the trees. It looked peaceful— unlike the disturbance currently in her mind.

Anna hated the silence between them. When they argued, it seemed like things would never go back to the easy banter they usually shared. But this wasn't her fault, and she didn't want to cave in.

Just when the silence became almost unbearable, she heard Dustin walking toward her again.

"I'm sorry," he said as he sat beside her. "I know you didn't mean for the door to close."

Her face softened. She scooted closer to him and rested her head on his shoulder. "What are we going to do?" she asked.

"Maybe we should start by eating something. We haven't eaten anything for a while. Then we can try to think it through."

As Dustin finished his sentence, she smelled Chinese food. "At least we won't starve here."

Dustin smiled at Anna. He got up and extended his hand to her. She took it, and he pulled her off the couch.

They walked to the table by the Big Kitchen, and Dustin pulled out a chair for her. Then he sat across from her.

"This cashew chicken is really good," Anna said.

"So is the egg drop soup."

As usual, all their favorites were there. But their predicament loomed over them, stifling their conversation. When they finished, Anna saw a plate on the island.

"What is that?" she asked.

Dustin walked over to get it. On the plate were two fortune cookies with their names on them. He cracked his open, pulled out the rectangular paper, and read:

In all your ways acknowledge Him,
and He shall direct your paths.

He raised his eyebrows. "What's that supposed to mean? Who is *Him*?"

"God," Anna said.

"How do you know that?"

"It's from Proverbs."

"Proverbs?"

"It's a verse from the Bible. I remember it from Sunday school."

"What does it mean?"

Anna shrugged. She didn't like that Dustin's cookie had a Bible verse in it. Fortune cookies were supposed to contain quirky sayings you could laugh at.

"What does yours say?" Dustin asked.

She opened it. The edges of the folded part of the cookie pinched the rectangular paper. When she yanked on it, it tore in two. Anna huffed and tossed it on the table.

Dustin picked it up, held the two pieces together, and read:

Whoever has no rule over his own spirit is like
a city broken down, without walls.

Anna rolled her eyes.

"Is that a Bible verse too?" Dustin asked.

"I don't know." Anna shoved her chair back and stood. "I'm done with this little game."

ANNA SAT on the couch by the Big Kitchen. The fortunes—which didn't seem like fortunes—irritated her. What was hers supposed to mean anyway? Her spirit was just fine.

Dustin sat beside her. "Are you okay?"

"Not really."

"I've been thinking about mine," he said. "Do you think the phrase *acknowledge Him* means we should pray?"

"I tried that once, and it didn't work."

Dustin pulled her close and put his arm around her. "Okay, let's not worry about what a piece of paper says. They're both gone now anyway."

"Did they disappear with the dishes?"

"They did."

"I don't know why that makes me feel better, but it does." Anna breathed deeply and put her head on his chest. His heartbeat soothed her.

"It'll be okay, Anna. We'll get through this together."

"If I had to be trapped with someone, I'm glad it's you." She relaxed her body against his. "Do you see that painting?" She pointed at *The Road to Chailly*.

"Your favorite Monet painting?"

She smiled. "You do pay attention."

"Sometimes."

"Do you think it means anything?"

"Maybe."

"Isn't it lovely? I feel mesmerized when I look at it."

"Honestly," Dustin said, "all I can think about now is getting out of here. Wherever *here* is."

Anna sat up. She felt like the moment was ruined. "So, do you have any ideas?"

"Not really. Do you?"

"We should eat cookies. And not those stupid fortune

cookie ones. A chocolate chip cookie would be great right now."

Anna looked down and grinned. A plate of freshly baked cookies had appeared on the coffee table. She picked one up and took a bite.

"Be serious, Anna. We need to figure out how to get out of here."

"I am being serious. This cookie is yummy."

Dustin frowned at her.

"Maybe we could take turns watching for the door," she said. "It might come back."

"Okay, I guess we can start with that. I'll take the first watch. There's no way I'd be able to sleep."

ANNA FOUND a bedroom close to the Big Kitchen. Soft light filtered through a skylight, and a large sleigh bed was adorned with just the right number of pillows. The bed sheets were soft, and the sage-green quilt, although not the color she would have chosen, was beautiful.

She looked in the closet. A pair of lavender pajamas hung there waiting for her. As she pulled them off the hanger, a glint of something on the floor caught her eye. She stooped and picked it up. It was a key of sorts. Bronze. Old. It looked like an antique skeleton key. The handle had an ornate fleur-de-lis pattern.

She put the key on the nightstand. Then she changed into the pajamas and slipped into bed. A fleeting thought of what the saying about her spirit meant passed through her mind, and then she fell asleep.

CHAPTER 11

Mary stood in the hallway, looking into JoJo's room. JoJo held a stuffed bear she had named Henry as Jim read her a story. The delight on their faces made Mary smile. JoJo pointed at something in the book, and Jim nodded. JoJo giggled.

Mary walked into the room and sat at the foot of the bed. She greeted them but received no response. She called out their names again. They continued with the story like she wasn't there.

"Okay, it's not funny anymore," Mary said. "You're starting to scare me."

She bounced on the bed and called their names over and over. Then she shouted out their names at the top of her lungs. The shout jolted her out of the dream state and into reality. Her body sprang up as another muffled cry escaped her throat.

She lay back on the couch, trying to hold on to their faces. But they had already faded. She lay with her eyes closed, trying to bring them back into focus.

And then she felt the heavy silence. Had she imagined the

storm? Was she back in that place? She slowly opened her eyes. No, she was in the man and woman's living room.

She hadn't realized she was holding her breath. Slowly exhaling, she walked to the den and opened the shutters. The storm had passed. A thick blanket of snow covered everything, sparkling in the bright sunlight. The view was amazing. No one had been out to mar the beautiful, white snow.

Mary closed the shutters and went into the kitchen. She prepared some strawberries and yogurt again and sat on a stool at the kitchen island.

Soon, she heard the plows clearing the street out front. And a soft whirr grew louder and then quieter. She went back to the den and looked out the window. A small plow had cleared the sidewalk. She watched as it returned and began clearing the driveway. As it got closer, she closed the shutter so the man wouldn't see her.

She listened as he cleared the driveway and then to the rhythmic scraping of a shovel on the front porch. After he finished, she heard him walking down the steps. She cracked open the shutter and watched him get into a truck and leave.

Mary opened the front door and looked out. The plows were gone; no one had come out of their houses yet. The cold, brisk air felt refreshing on her face. She stood there for a moment and then closed the door.

Relieved, she went back to finish her breakfast. As she ate, she picked up the yogurt cup. She had never heard of the brand, but it was good—thick, creamy, and smooth. With the fresh strawberries, it was delicious.

Then she turned the cup over and saw writing on the bottom: "best by Apr 11 2021."

Mary stared at it in disbelief. Could that be right? Maybe she had read it wrong. It *had* to be wrong.

A feeling of dread washed over her. Had she been gone for *thirty* years? It was either incorrect or she was misreading it. No way. It wasn't possible.

Mary's head swam. She couldn't think straight. How could it be 2021? That would make her sixty-one years old.

Mary looked at herself in the full-length mirror. Even objectively, she didn't look like she was sixty-one. She had about the same number of wrinkles as when she left. There were no gray strands in her hair. Besides the length of her hair, she looked pretty much like she did the day she went through the door. 2021. How could that be?

She began searching for confirmation of *when* she was. She needed to find something better than a yogurt cup to verify the date. There weren't any newspapers or magazines lying around. Nor was there a calendar on the wall. She couldn't even find a radio.

She decided that the mirror-like thing on the wall in the living room was a fancy TV. But she couldn't find any buttons on it or a remote to turn it on.

As Mary tried to think of what else she could look for to confirm the date, the doorbell clanged in her ears. She held her breath, hoping whoever it was would go away. After a minute, she exhaled and started to move.

Ding-dong! They were persistent—whoever *they* were. Mary stood still, listening for the footfalls of them leaving.

Instead, she heard a key in the lock. Her heart raced as she hid behind the sofa. She tried to quiet her breathing. From her vantage point, she could look around the edge of the couch and see the front door.

"Hello?" a man said. "Is anyone home?"

An older couple stepped in and paused. Then they took off their boots and walked down the hallway.

"I thought they were only supposed to be gone for a couple of days," the woman said.

They both looked like they were in their late sixties. Her

white hair was clipped short, and curls framed her face. A belt held in his middle. He walked cautiously as if any sudden movement would end badly.

The woman put a vase of flowers on the kitchen island, and the man placed a card beside it.

"Well," he said, "they'll see it when they get back."

"You'd think they would have cleaned up before they left." She smirked and picked up the yogurt cup. "And look at the blankets on the couch. They aren't even folded." The woman started walking toward the living room.

"Now, Martha, don't start cleaning up. I'm sure they'll get to it when they come home."

"Fine. But who does that? I didn't raise him like that."

"Let's go. It's their house."

Mary watched the couple walk down the hallway and put on their boots. The man opened the front door for Martha. She walked through it, and he followed. She heard the key in the lock, and then it was silent.

Mary let out a sigh of relief. She walked to the front door and looked out the window beside it. Martha and the man got into a car and drove away.

She closed the shutter and walked down the hallway to the kitchen. The card was sealed but didn't have anything written on the outside. The flowers were lovely; their fragrance filled the room.

She couldn't help but think of the wildflowers she had seen outside the windows on the other side of the door. They filled the landscape. She often imagined how they would smell.

Then she went back to the front door. She twisted the deadbolt and pushed down on the bronze lever. As the door opened, she felt the cold air on her face. She went out and stood on the porch, watching the wind rush through the trees. She shivered. She was chilly, but she didn't want to go inside.

The house cast a shadow on the snow-covered lawn. She closed her eyes and enjoyed the fresh air.

After her fingers grew cold, she went inside. The icy air had reached her bones. She thought about looking for a coat so she could stay outside longer. Instead, she decided to explore and try to confirm when she was.

Mary walked to the living room to look for clues. The man and the woman who had gone through the door smiled at her from the frames on the fireplace mantel—moments frozen in time. The woman was beautiful.

She spotted a picture of a family. Did they have kids? She held the frame so she could examine the photograph. As she looked at it, she gasped.

It was a picture of her, her husband, and their little girl. Tears streamed down her face. What was her picture doing here?

The sound of breaking glass startled Mary. Looking down, she saw jagged pieces of glass at her feet. She hadn't felt the picture slip from her fingers.

Mary stooped. The smooth, wooden frame, *her* picture frame, was still intact. But the glass had shattered.

She picked up the familiar picture and stood. On the back, there was a date in her handwriting: June 20, 1990. That had been a great day. A day that seemed like a lifetime ago.

Mary stared at the photo of their California vacation—cheerful faces on the beach at sunset, a self-portrait. Jim was good at taking those. They ate dinner at one of those Hawaiian-themed restaurants. She could still hear the luau music on the patio and feel the warm breeze on her face. JoJo giggled at a dad joke. They strolled on the beach, and then Jim captured the moment with this photograph.

She pushed back the memory. She needed to find something to clean up the glass. But the questions raced through her mind. Why was the picture here? And where were her husband and daughter now?

MARY SAT on a stool at the kitchen island and propped up the photograph on the base of the flower vase. She rested her head in the crook of her elbow and stared at it. Goose bumps rose on her arms as the cold from the granite seeped into her skin. But she kept her head where it was, gazing at their faces on that day long ago.

She thought if she came back through the door, she would return to the same place. But this was *not* her house.

It had a similar floor plan. But in hers, a wall separated the living room from the kitchen. And none of her furniture was there. Even the countertops and cabinets were different.

She was tired. As she gazed at the picture, she imagined what JoJo would look like now. Her daughter was only seven years old when she went through the door. How would she look at thirty-seven? But the daylight was growing dim, and their faces were indistinguishable.

Mary got up and put the photo in the patch pocket of her sweater. She walked back to the front door and stepped outside. Then she sat on the front step and watched the world grow dark.

CHAPTER 12

Dustin sat on a stool in the Big Kitchen, looking at the wall where the door should have been. Although Anna's idea wasn't a bad one, there had to be another way out of there. He had wanted to discuss it with her—to brainstorm ideas—but there was no talking to her when she got upset like that.

And then he had an idea: he would make a doorway. If their kitchen were on the other side, maybe they could get to it if he broke through the wall.

He searched through the cabinets and drawers for something he could use. The meat tenderizer? No, not substantial enough. A hammer? That would work better, but it wouldn't do enough damage.

He was almost ready to give up. But when he opened the pantry, a sledgehammer was sitting on the shelf. He smiled. He took the sledgehammer over to the wall, estimated where the door had been, and swung.

A LOUD BOOM interrupted Anna's sleep. She sprang up and listened. She only heard silence. But as she lay back on the pillow, the boom resounded again.

She followed the noise. As she walked toward the Big Kitchen, she saw Dustin surrounded by a cloud of dust. His jaw clenched as he swung a sledgehammer. Blow after blow sent drywall and wood flying in every direction. *The Road to Chailly* hung askew on the wall.

"Dustin!" She yelled his name four times before he turned toward her. "What are you doing?"

"I'm trying to find the door."

"Where did you get a sledgehammer?"

"It was over there in that pantry."

As they talked, she watched the wall. It was putting itself back together. She pointed at it. "Look."

Dustin turned. He frowned and continued his blows. No matter how many times he swung the sledgehammer, there was more drywall. And boards. He was getting nowhere.

Anna turned and left. She would let him get his frustration out. As she lay in bed listening, she grew accustomed to the sound and fell back asleep.

DUSTIN STARED AT THE WALL. It looked like nothing had happened. There wasn't even any dust on the floor.

He glanced at the sledgehammer leaning against the island. He felt like it was good to have tried. At least now, he knew that wouldn't work and could move on to something else. But he didn't have any other ideas. Yet.

He tried to calculate how long they had been there. It had been about three days in actual time when they discovered the door was gone. They planned their trip so they would only be gone that long. But with the shock of it all, their argument, and everything else, he lost track of how he could *sense* the passage of time before. Maybe another three days had passed? Maybe longer?

He didn't think it had been a full week. If the door followed its previous pattern of showing up on Mondays, there should be time to shower without missing its return—that is, *if* it returned.

Unlike the room, he was filthy. Sweat and grime from the drywall dust covered his face and arms. He walked down the hallway and found a suite with a bathroom.

A towel waited for him, along with soap, shampoo, and a washcloth in the walk-in shower. He could see a change of clothes in the adjoining closet. *This place thinks of everything.*

CLEAN AND REFRESHED, Dustin walked to the Big Kitchen, thinking about coffee. He was exhausted. But he didn't want to sleep until Anna got up. As he passed by the bedroom where Anna slept, he looked in. Her sleep looked restless.

Dustin continued down the hallway and found a mug of hot coffee on the kitchen island. He took it to a recliner where he could watch the wall. Although he tried to focus on coming up with another way of escaping this place, he couldn't help thinking about the fortune cookie paper.

What did it say? Something about acknowledging Him and directing a path? Anna said it was a Bible verse from Proverbs. That much he remembered. He wondered if he should look it up.

WHEN ANNA AWOKE, she felt agitated. She didn't like sleeping without Dustin beside her. His presence had a calming effect.

She found him in a chair by the Big Kitchen—snoring. His head was twisted at a weird angle, but she let him sleep. He hadn't slept since they got there. If she woke him to try to get him to go to bed, he might not be able to go back to sleep.

The room looked serene. She saw no evidence of Dustin's attempt to break through the wall, and *The Road to Chailly* continued to invite her to spend an afternoon walking along its path.

She turned and saw another plate of fresh cookies on the kitchen island. She hadn't eaten that many cookies since . . . well, she didn't think she'd ever eaten that many. For some reason, they sounded like just the right thing.

She sat on a stool and stared at the wall. As she watched, her mind waffled between focusing on how good the cookies were and her mom.

"Are you eating *another* cookie?"

She looked up and saw Dustin grinning at her. She smiled; she loved how his whole face lit up when he teased her.

"Yes. Yes, I am. They're kind of irresistible. Besides, with the whole time-differential thing, I'm guessing calories must burn more quickly too."

Dustin laughed and grabbed a chocolate chip cookie. "I like your logic."

"It's weird how they keep showing up. And they're always so warm and soft."

"Yeah, if we're stuck here much longer, I'm going to lose my beautiful physique. I think I've already gained ten pounds." He looked at Anna and sat on a stool beside her. "But seriously, you were a million miles away just now. Are you okay?"

"I was thinking about my mom."

Dustin reached out and took her hand.

"It was bizarre—like she just vanished, you know? Her purse, wallet, keys, car—everything was still at our house. But she wasn't there."

"That must have been so hard for you."

"I don't remember much about it. The school bus dropped

me off, and when I . . ." Anna gazed into the distance. "But you know, it was the strangest thing. As I crossed the road, I saw a man running out of our house and down the street. He had a huge beard and long hair. It really creeped me out."

"You never told me that before."

"I went to Mrs. Garwood's house. She walked with me to our house, but no one was there. Mom was already gone."

"Did they ever find the man?"

"No. They said I made it up." Anna grimaced. "But I didn't. I know what I saw." Tears welled up in her eyes. "It's silly to cry after all this time."

"It's not silly. I understand."

"Mrs. Garwood called my dad. When he got home, he searched the house. Because her purse and car were still there, he called the police. They never did find any evidence of what happened to her."

She brushed the tears from her cheeks.

"The accusations against my dad were awful. The police cleared him of any wrongdoing. But I heard whispers for years saying my dad did something to her."

Dustin squeezed her hand.

"It's not fair. My mom wasn't there for my high school dances, graduation, or our wedding. And we still don't know what happened to her."

Dustin took her into his arms and held her. She felt another tear escape her eye, travel around her cheekbone, and down to her chin.

"Did I ever tell you that I prayed that night?"

"No."

"I did. And God didn't answer. It felt like I lost both my mom and God that night. Why didn't He answer?"

CHAPTER 13

Mary kept her eyes closed as she woke up. She heard the faint sound of a car passing and a bird squawking. Then she remembered everything that had happened.

She lay there, planning her next course of action. She needed to confirm *when* she was. After that, she could try to figure out where she had ended up. But first, she would eat something.

As Mary reached into the refrigerator to grab the eggs, the doorbell rang. She stopped and listened. After a minute, she heard a key in the lock and the front door open.

"Dustin? Are you home?"

Mary recognized Martha's voice. She decided to confront her instead of hiding. Mary walked around the corner and saw Martha stooped over, taking off her boots.

"Hi, I'm Mary. Who are you?"

Martha turned toward Mary and lifted her eyebrows. "I'm Martha, Dustin's mom. What are you doing here?" Her expression soured. She gave Mary the I-belong-here-but-you-don't look.

"I'm housesitting. They found a travel deal they couldn't resist. It was a spur-of-the-moment kind of thing."

"Oh." Martha's face softened a little. But she looked like she wasn't quite ready to give up.

"I'll let them know you dropped by when they get back," Mary said.

"Okay." Martha started putting her boots on.

"Could you leave the key?" Mary asked. "You really gave me a start. I'll leave it with them to give back to you when I'm done housesitting."

Martha studied Mary as she took the key off the ring and handed it to her.

"Thanks." Mary took the key and ushered Martha out the front door. As she closed the door and locked it, she exhaled slowly. *That's a relief.*

MARY CONTINUED SEARCHING for a date written on something more reliable than a yogurt cup. As she looked in the den for a calendar, she found a few pieces of unopened mail on the desk. She took a deep breath and looked at the postmark: "Mar 26 2021." That seemed to confirm it. She still couldn't believe it had been that long.

And then something else caught her eye. The envelope was addressed to Dustin Hughes. But the address, 425 Parkwood Lane . . . that was hers.

It took a minute to sink in. The house looked so different. Yet, despite the changes, it was the same one.

She set the envelope down and pulled the photograph from her sweater pocket. The smiling face of her six-year-old daughter stared back at her. Could the woman she saw be JoJo?

Mary went to the living room and picked up a picture of the woman. She studied her features and compared them to the photo in her pocket. The smile was the same, and so was the shape of her nose and chin.

She had missed so much time. Anna Josephine. Had she kept her last name, Bauer? Or was it Anna Josephine Hughes now?

A tear rolled down her cheek. She didn't see her beautiful girl transform into this lovely woman. She missed birthdays, Christmases, her graduation, and her wedding. She hadn't been there to listen and give her advice. She missed those moments of comforting Anna in the hard times, encouraging her, and cheering her on. Deep regret gripped Mary's heart.

But then she chastised herself. *It won't do any good to wallow in what I've lost. I can't go back—no matter how much I want to.*

MARY PUT the picture back on the mantel. She decided to investigate. She walked through the rooms again, looking for evidence of her house from thirty years ago.

The wood flooring was the same. She remembered the pattern of the maple. But the rest had been redone. All the furniture had been replaced. Even the kitchen cabinets and countertops were different.

Yet, as she opened the door to the basement, she was met with the familiar wooden staircase painted a steel-grey color. She walked down the stairs. At the bottom was the bathroom Jim had added. Except for the bathroom, the basement was still unfinished. The concrete spread over the single, open space.

Anna and Dustin had continued using it for storage. She walked by cardboard boxes stacked on the metal shelving Jim had set up to keep them off the floor. She scanned the boxes and noticed a few labeled "Mom's stuff." She sighed. Had her entire life been reduced to a couple of boxes?

Mary pulled down a box, set it on an empty table, and

peeled back the packing tape. As she opened the cardboard flaps, she saw her favorite sweater. The sweater was worn and tattered in places, but she loved it. Jim had teased her whenever she wore it. He said she looked like a hobo because of the small holes in the front and on the elbows.

Under the sweater were her journals—dozens of them neatly stacked. She had dreamt of being a writer one day. Book ideas, prose, scenes from various stories, and character sketches filled them. They smelled musty. It was strange to think it had been long enough for them to begin to decompose. She thought of her time on the other side of the door. Now, that would make a good story.

She opened another box filled with photo albums. She flipped through one and saw Jim looking back at her. His wavy brown hair and blue eyes melted her heart. Tears streamed down her cheeks. The pages were filled with pictures of her and Jim.

Her eyes were drawn to a photo of Jim on Christmas morning. They had gotten up before sunrise to wrap presents before going to his parents' house. She snapped the picture because he looked sneaky as he wrapped one of the gifts. The photo captured the impish glint in his eyes. He had been up to something.

Later that day, he handed her the gift with that same twinkle in his eyes. As she unwrapped the small box, she found a key—the key to this house. He knew how much she loved it. So, he bought it for them to start their family.

They went through the empty rooms and dreamt about how they would furnish each one. They talked about having children and picked out which room would be the nursery.

What happened to Jim? Mary closed the album and set it down. This wasn't the time to reminisce. She had the confirmation she sought. And now she had to think it through. She had to figure out how to set things right.

Mary sat at the dining room table, facing the wall—as if by staring at it, she could somehow will the door to return. What if it didn't come back? The thought made her cringe. How could she have shut her daughter in that place? What kind of mother was she? First, to be gone all those years. And then to possibly subject her daughter to the same fate?

She reached into her pocket and pulled out a gold earring. Somehow, she had lost the other one. She turned it in her hand and looked at the diamond, sapphire, and emerald stones—the birthstones for her, Jim, and JoJo. It was a link to her former life.

Mary put the earring back in her pocket. She couldn't make the door come back. But she could be vigilant and watch for its return, so she wouldn't miss it if it did.

CHAPTER 14

Anna watched as Dustin's eyes closed for increasingly longer intervals. His hand had been propping up his head. But when his eyes remained shut for almost fifteen seconds, his head slid off his hand, and his eyes flashed open.

"You should lie down and get some sleep," Anna said.

"I slept."

"Yeah, maybe for fifteen minutes."

"Isn't that like more than an hour in our time?"

"If you sleep a little, you'll think better. Besides, if you don't get some rest now, you might not be able to stay awake when I go to sleep later."

"Okay, I'll try. But it seems like you're trying to get rid of me."

Anna smiled. "I am. So I can eat more cookies without you being all judgy about it."

"Judgy isn't a word."

"Yes, it is. I used it, and you knew exactly what I meant."

Dustin grinned at her. "If you say so."

He kissed her cheek and walked down the hallway. When

he was gone, she picked up another cookie and took a bite. She sat on a stool, looking at the wall and thinking.

What if the door doesn't come back? Could we be trapped here forever? What if our marriage isn't strong enough to withstand this? The questions flooded her mind. It was annoying. But they came one after another. She couldn't get her mind to stop.

Anna felt her mind slipping—tottering on a precipice and ready to fall into the abyss at any moment. She needed something to distract her. She didn't want to miss the door if it came back. But surely a quick trip to the library wouldn't hurt.

She hurried down the main hallway, around the curve, and into the library. She pushed the ladder around to where she had found the book before, climbed it, and pulled out *Sense and Sensibility*. She tucked it under her arm and headed back.

As she rounded the corner to the Big Kitchen, she thought she saw a door closing out of the corner of her eye. But when she looked up, she only saw a wall and *The Road to Chailly*.

She sat in a recliner, reading the last half of the book. Every few minutes, she glanced up at the wall, looking for the door.

The Dashwood sisters seemed resilient. Their change in circumstances had been difficult, but they soldiered on, working their way through each challenge. Of course, they didn't have to deal with being trapped in—whatever this place was. Maybe she should be reading *The Lion, the Witch, and the Wardrobe* instead.

In the end, everything was neatly wrapped up for the Dashwood sisters. Both Elinor and Marianne married and lived contented lives as neighbors. She closed the book and set it on the coffee table.

As she did, the window in the Big Kitchen caught her eye. She walked over to it. The view was the same—purple, pink, yellow, and white flowers dotted the landscape. But she had never looked at the window itself.

She studied it but saw no evidence that it opened. There

weren't any grooves or tracks for the window to slide on. It was comprised of a single pane of glass in a single frame. Why didn't it open? Was the air outside toxic? Or was this some kind of prison?

DUSTIN WOKE UP, thinking about the paper in his fortune cookie. He couldn't figure out what it meant. But he knew he could use some direction.

He got up, dressed, and went to find Anna. He found her looking at the window in the Big Kitchen. Her hand moved over the frame as she frowned.

"Good morning," Dustin said.

"It always looks like it's morning."

"What are you doing?"

"Have you noticed that the window doesn't open?"

"I don't think any of them do."

"It would be nice to go for a walk outside." She turned to Dustin and hugged him. "Sorry, I was preoccupied. Did you sleep?"

"A bit."

"Good. Have you looked at the other windows?"

"Before we got trapped here, I looked at them when we came to explore. I didn't see any that open. They all look like this one."

"That's weird," she said. "Why wouldn't they open?"

"I don't know."

"It makes me feel even more confined."

"Maybe it's for our own good?"

"What does that mean?"

"Just that, maybe it wouldn't be safe for us to go outside."

"I'm feeling tired," Anna said. "I think I'm going to go lie down for a while."

After Anna left, Dustin went to the library to get the Bible she had shown him the first time he was there with her. He pulled out a book. *Clear and Present Danger*, by Tom Clancy. It was old, but he'd been wanting to read it. He had been going through some of the older Jack Ryan books. He made a mental note to come back for it later.

The next book he pulled out was a Bible. He hurried down the ladder, took it back to the Big Kitchen, and sat on a stool.

Anna said the verse was from Proverbs. He opened the Bible and found the table of contents. There were a lot of "books" in the Bible. He scanned the page and finally found it: Proverbs was on page 831.

After going through the first two chapters, he sighed. He had hoped to find it quickly. He turned through the pages to see how long the Book of Proverbs was. Thirty-one chapters. It was a good thing he didn't have anything else to do.

In chapter three, he found it. And it had other words in the same sentence. The entire saying was:

> *Trust in the LORD with all your heart,*
> *and lean not on your own understanding;*
> *in all your ways acknowledge Him,*
> *and He shall direct your paths.*

He remembered Anna saying it referred to God. That made sense. He had never really thought about God, and he didn't know how to trust God or acknowledge Him. But he decided to pray. It couldn't hurt, right?

He folded his hands like he'd seen others do and bowed his head. "God, if you can hear me, we could use your help. I don't know what to do to get us out of here. Please help us."

"What are you doing?"

Dustin jumped. "Don't sneak up on me like that."

"Yeah, that's me, stealthy like a four-month-old puppy chasing a squeaky toy on linoleum."

Dustin frowned at her.

"What?" Anna said. "I'm just saying you were focused."

Dustin ignored her. He picked up a ruler and drew a line.

"What is it?" Anna asked.

"A map."

Anna looked over Dustin's shoulder at the poster-board-sized drawing paper. He had started with the landmarks they had discovered: the Big Kitchen, the den, the library, the pool, and the music room. He connected them, showing some of the twists and turns in the main path and on the smaller paths they had traveled.

"Why?" she asked.

"Why what?"

"Why are you making a map?"

"I'm putting down everything we know about this place so we can see it differently. Maybe it will help us to find a way home."

Anna wrinkled her forehead. "How's that going to make the door come back?"

"It won't. But maybe there's a different way to get out of here."

"It seems like a waste of time."

"Do you have a better idea?"

"No."

"That's what I thought."

CHAPTER 15

The next few days dragged on as Mary sat at the table, staring at the wall. She alternated between sitting and walking around the kitchen. She reminisced about JoJo and Jim. She ate yogurt, leftover pizza, and sandwiches. Her supplies were starting to get low.

She thought about the refrigerators on the other side of the door. She had grown used to how they magically replenished themselves. They were always well-stocked. Before long, she would need to figure out how to get money to buy food.

At some point, she fell asleep hunched over the table with her head on her arms. She woke up with light streaming through the shutters. And there it was. The door had returned.

Mary sprang up and ran to the door. She took a deep breath and pushed down on the bronze lever.

As she opened the door, she surveyed what she could see. The hallway stretched out before her. The living space by the Big Kitchen was empty. No one was there. She called out JoJo's name, but there was no response. She couldn't hear any noise from the other side.

Mary hesitated. What if she went in to look for them and

the door closed? Then they'd all be trapped. She shuddered at the thought.

Maybe she should leave the door open, but stay on this side of it. That seemed like the better plan. Eventually, they would return to the Big Kitchen and see the open doorway. Mary opened the door until she felt the bronze lever touch the wall.

But as she stepped back to sit on a dining room chair, she felt a gust of air as the door slammed. Eyes wide, she jumped, and her heart raced. What had just happened?

She shook her head. The door had closed of its own volition. Why didn't it stay open? Is that how she got trapped there? But then, why did it stay open for her to come back this last time?

The door had vanished. The wall was just a wall again, with two windows and no door. She sat at the table, trying to think it through. And then she heard the doorbell.

She went into the den and peeked out of a shutter. An older woman stood in front of the door wearing a puffy coat with a cat in her arms. Her hair was pulled back. A few chestnut brown strands stood out amidst the white ones. Although her scarf partially covered her chin, she looked a lot like an older version of her friend, Lydia.

Mary smiled as she opened the door.

"Hello, dear," the woman said. "And who might you be?"

"I'm Mary. I'm housesitting."

"Oh, that's lovely. I just came over to see how Anna and Dustin were faring with this snowstorm. I live in that house over there."

It was definitely Lydia. "Would you like to come in?"

"That would be delightful. I'll just warm up a bit, and then I'll be on my way. That icy wind cuts right through you."

Mrs. Garwood held the cat under her arm while she took off her boots. Then she followed Mary to the kitchen.

"I'd offer you some coffee," Mary said, "but I haven't figured out how to work their machine."

"Oh, I can show you, dear." The cat jumped out of her arms, and Mrs. Garwood opened a drawer. "You just pop one of these little pods in here, close it, and push this button."

"I'll get us some mugs."

While Mary made them coffee, Mrs. Garwood sat at the kitchen table.

"Would you like cream or sugar?" Mary asked.

"Sugar, no cream."

Mary brought the mugs of coffee and the sugar on a tray.

"Thank you, dear."

The cat bounced and tried to catch his tail. But when he got close to the wall where the door had been, he arched his back and hissed.

Mrs. Garwood laughed. "He's a good kitty, but he's a bit nutty."

"He's pretty funny." *And perceptive.* "What's his name?"

"Max."

"That's a great name for a cat."

"You know," Mrs. Garwood said, "I can't put my finger on it, but you look familiar. You remind me of someone I used to know."

"Maybe I'm her doppelganger?"

Max jumped into Mrs. Garwood's lap, looked back at the wall, and hissed again.

"How long are you staying here?"

"Just until they get back."

"Well, I'm glad they were able to get away. They work so hard."

"Do you live alone?"

"I'm sure they told you. It's just me and Max. My Will passed away—it's been almost ten years now."

"I'm sorry to hear that." Mary frowned. Will was dead? How many other things had changed? She felt sad for her friend. Will and Lydia had been a fun couple to be around. They had met weekly for a game night, usually cribbage.

"How do you know Dustin and Anna?" Mrs. Garwood asked.

Mary tried to look nonchalant. "Oh, we go way back. I can't even remember when I met them."

Mrs. Garwood raised her eyebrows ever so slightly and tilted her head. Mary could tell she didn't believe her. But instead of pursuing it, Mrs. Garwood changed the subject. "Did you hear? It's supposed to snow again tonight."

"I hadn't heard. I haven't been able to find the TV remote."

Mrs. Garwood smiled. "I'm feeling pretty toasty now. Max and I should be getting home." She stood with Max in her arms and headed toward the front door. Max looked at the wall again and hissed.

Mary followed Mrs. Garwood. "Do you want me to hold Max while you put your boots on?"

"Oh, thank you. That would be helpful."

Mary took Max in her arms and rubbed his ears. Max purred. When Mrs. Garwood had her boots on, she handed Max back.

"Get home safely," Mary said. "I don't think you told me your name."

"It's Lydia, dear. Lydia Garwood."

"Thanks for dropping by, Lydia. It was a pleasure talking with you."

Mary watched as her old friend carefully made her way down the steps. Mrs. Garwood walked along the sidewalk to her house and then up the steps to her doorway. When she was safe inside, Mary closed the door as a tear slid down her cheek.

CHAPTER 16

Anna lay on the bed, staring at the ceiling. Its design made it look like it was vaulted. Earlier, she had stood on the bed and could easily touch it. She was trying to figure out how the illusion worked.

Originally, she chose the room because of its proximity to the Big Kitchen. But after being in it, she decided she liked it a lot. For one, it was perfectly square. And when you were lying on the large bed, the door was on your right.

Its layout also intrigued her. At first, it didn't look like it had an attached bathroom. Yet, when you stood to the left of the closet and looked at just the right angle, you could see the entrance to a narrow hallway. That hallway led to a sprawling bathroom—one bigger than the bedroom itself.

The only thing she hadn't cared for was the color of the quilt. But after thinking that, the quilt had changed to a soft lilac the next time she returned.

As she stared at the ceiling, she heard Dustin's voice.

"Are you getting out of bed today?"

"What's today? It's always today."

"You know what I mean, Anna. You've been in here a long time."

"How long have I been in here?"

"You know I don't know exactly. Are you getting up or not?"

"Not."

Anna heard Dustin leave the room. When he was gone, she looked at the door. He had left it open. It irritated her, but she didn't want to get up to close it.

She returned her mind to the ceiling puzzle. If she didn't focus on something, her thoughts would start spiraling down again. And if they went too far, she might be lost.

***

"OH, HEY, YOU'RE UP," Dustin said. "Come look at this."

Anna looked at the island where Dustin sat on a stool. His eyes sparkled as he pointed at the paper in front of him. She shuffled over and sat beside him. The map he had been working on was more intricate than when she had last seen it.

"So?" she said.

"As I was working on this, I realized something. Do you remember the day we tried to see if we could find the end of the first smaller hallway?"

"What about it?"

"I saw a peculiar desk close to where we turned around." He pointed at the map. "It was right about here."

"I remember. It had lion head carvings and other designs, like grapevines or something."

"That's the one. Well, when we walked down the main hallway the last time, I saw the same desk before we turned around."

"You didn't say anything."

"It didn't register at the time."

"So what?" Anna said. "There are two weird desks."

"I think it's the same desk."

"I don't get it."

Dustin took the bottom of the paper and pulled the left and right sides together. "I think the main hallway and the first smaller one are the same. They form a sort of loop."

"How will that bring the door back?" She watched Dustin. He was deep in thought and didn't answer her question. A few minutes later, he looked up at her and grinned.

"Should we test it?" he asked.

"Test what?"

"My map theory."

"What if the door comes back while we're gone?"

"I don't think it will. Remember how it only appeared on Mondays? I don't think it's been a full week yet." He bit the corner of his lip as he said it. He was lying; that was his tell.

"That could change," Anna said. "The door never closed before either."

"I think we need to find out more about this place so we can come up with some way to get out of here."

She could tell he wasn't going to give up on this one. Of course, she could stay and let him check out the theory by himself. But she didn't want them to split up.

"Okay," Anna said. "Let's go see if you're right."

<hr>

Dustin rolled up his map and put a pencil in his pocket. "Ready?" he asked.

Anna nodded.

"Let's go down the smaller hallway, so we'll get to the desk quicker."

He led them down the hallway. As they walked, she was surprised that she recognized different rooms. Before, the rooms seemed to meld together, one after another. Now, she could more readily distinguish between them. There was the den, the smaller kitchen they had eaten lunch in, the octagon-shaped room, and the room with the bed that had curtains around it.

When they were hungry, they stopped to eat Jersey-style pizza and cold root beer in frosty mugs. The crispy, thin crust was almost burned on the bottom, and the pizza sauce mingled with the grease from the pepperoni. She felt like she was back in the corner pizza shop they had stumbled upon while visiting Dustin's uncle in Pennsylvania.

She smiled at Dustin. The food gave way to conversation. Lately, it seemed they argued every time they talked. But this was different. Their conversation wasn't forced and stilted; it was warm and congenial. She felt like they were on the same page again.

"LET'S KEEP GOING," Dustin said. "It shouldn't be much farther."

They pushed in their chairs and started down the hallway again. There was a room with exercise bikes in it that she hadn't noticed before. Then, as they rounded a corner, she saw the desk in the distance.

The desk was peculiar, more so than she remembered. On each corner, a carved image of a lion stared back as if challenging them. One corner had a lion roaring, its ferocious teeth almost glinting in the soft light. On another, the lion's mouth was closed. A third lion's head was turned away, but its eyes looked back, piercing through them. And a fourth lifted its head with a proud gaze.

"It looks eerie, doesn't it?" Anna stepped closer and reached out to touch it, half expecting one of the lion heads to bite off her hand.

The smooth cherry wood had an elaborate grapevine carved around the edge. Inset satinwood and boxwood created opulent designs. Further inspection revealed several pigeonholes and drawers. A fountain pen and an inkwell lay beside some linen stationery, ready for someone to pen a letter.

As they examined the desk, Dustin pointed to a keyhole on the front toward the top. "I wonder where the key is."

Anna looked. The keyhole was in a band of wood that looked fixed. And then she remembered the key she found in the bedroom closet. She pulled it out of her front pocket and handed it to Dustin.

"Do you think this might open it?" she asked.

"Where did you get that?"

"I found it earlier."

"Well, we might as well try it."

The key was a perfect fit. When Dustin turned it, a secret compartment popped out of the side. The edges of the three-by-three-inch hidden drawer were unfinished.

Dustin carefully pulled out the drawer. The drawer was long—too long to support itself when it was all the way out. It was the perfect size for a scroll, and that's exactly what was in it. Anna carefully removed the three-foot-long scroll from the drawer. After Dustin pushed the drawer back into the desk, she handed it to him.

"Let's go over to that table and open it." He pointed to four small paperweights on the desk. "Bring those."

Anna picked up the paperweights and followed Dustin. She turned the small spheres in her hands. Each was flattened slightly on one side. And each was made from a different type of stone: marble, granite, quartz, and amethyst. The amethyst was a deep purple. She liked that one the best.

Dustin unfurled the parchment on the table, and she placed a paperweight on each corner. It was a map. It looked old, but the parchment was new. At the top, she saw a date written in a calligraphic font: 1901.

Dustin opened his map and placed it beside the parchment. The general structure was similar. And it depicted the space in the way Dustin suggested—in a loop.

Although the configuration of the hallways generally looked the same, the names of the rooms were somewhat different. There was a map key with numbers corresponding to the different rooms. The library was still the library. But there was a drawing room where their music room had been. And instead of a pool, there was an indoor garden.

"What would an indoor garden look like?" Anna asked.

Dustin didn't answer. Anna wondered if he had even heard her. His finger moved over the map as he studied it.

Anna looked back at the map. It was detailed. The line depicting the smaller hallway they had just walked down seemed to account for the tiniest variation. Her eyes followed the line back toward the Big Kitchen, which was labeled with a 3. When she looked at the key, she saw it was called the Main Kitchen.

She was intrigued by the idea that someone had been here in 1901 and that things were different then. When did it change? And why?

Anna put her hand on Dustin's arm. He looked up at her, and she pointed at the desk.

"Did you notice that the desk doesn't look like anything else?" Anna asked. "Not just in this room but every other room we've been in?"

"Yeah, not even remotely."

"Do you think it could be a sort of holdover from 1901?"

"Maybe the desk stayed because of its contents," he said.

"The map?"

"Exactly."

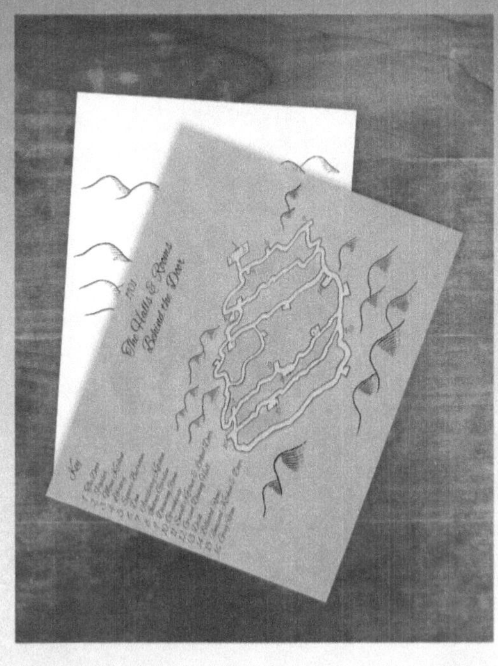

Discover the world beyond Anna's magical door!

Claim your FREE maps to help you navigate the mysterious realm alongside Anna and Dustin.

Scan the QR code

OR go to:

https://catherine-mcdaugale.kit.com/the_door_maps

CHAPTER 17

Mary lay on the couch, trying to think of a reason to get up, when the doorbell rang. She hoped it wasn't Martha again. Then she connected the dots: if Martha was Dustin's mom and Anna was married to Dustin, Martha was an in-law. *Yikes. Well, I'm sure she's nice once you get to know her.*

Mary looked through the peephole on the door and saw Mrs. Garwood with Max tucked in her puffy coat. She unlocked the door and opened it.

"Good morning, Mary dear. I wasn't sure if you were an early riser or a late one. I hope I didn't wake you."

"Please, come in out of the cold."

She took Max while Mrs. Garwood removed her boots and coat.

"Do you want me to hang up your coat?"

"Oh, no need to fuss. It'll be fine right here on the banister."

Mary led Mrs. Garwood down the hallway. "Would you like some coffee?"

"That would be lovely. It'll warm up the insides."

As Mary brought the coffee to the table, Max stood by the wall, arching his back and hissing.

"I don't know what's gotten into him," Mrs. Garwood said. "Well, never mind that goofy kitty. How are you doing?"

"Oh, fine." Mary sipped her coffee. Instead of, *Oh, fine,* she wanted to say, *Don't you recognize me, Lydia? It's me, Mary.*

And then she heard Mrs. Garwood exclaim, "Where did that door come from?"

Mary looked up. The door was back.

"You can see it?" Mary said.

"Of course, it's right there, plain as day."

Mary walked over to it. As soon as she opened the door, Max shot through it and ran down the main hallway out of sight.

"Max!"

Mrs. Garwood started to follow him, but Mary caught her arm and pulled her back.

"Wait," Mary said. "Max will be okay. Let me explain."

Mary peered through the door but saw no sign of Anna or Dustin. She opened it as far as it would go. Then she gestured to Mrs. Garwood to sit down.

After they were seated, the door slammed. Mrs. Garwood jumped, and Mary watched as the door disappeared into the wall.

When the door was gone, Mary looked at her friend. Mrs. Garwood sat upright. Her hands shook, and her cheeks were flushed. She took in quick, shallow breaths.

"Lydia, are you okay?" Mary put her hand on Mrs. Garwood's shoulder.

"What just happened?"

"It's hard to explain."

"What am I going to do?" Mrs. Garwood's eyes darted between Mary and the wall where the door had been. "Is Max going to be alright? What happened to him?"

"I know it doesn't make sense right now. But I promise we'll get him back."

Mary kept her hand on her friend's shoulder until her breathing slowed. When Mrs. Garwood was calm, Mary looked at her and said, "Lydia, it's me, Mary."

"Yes, dear, I know your name is Mary."

"No, it's me. Your friend from thirty years ago. JoJo's mom. Do you remember me?" Mary pulled the old photograph of her, Jim, and Anna out of her pocket and gave it to Mrs. Garwood.

Mrs. Garwood's face paled, and her mouth gaped. Mary gave her time to process. She squinted at the photograph and then at Mary, alternating between them.

A few minutes later, Mrs. Garwood handed the photo to Mary and stood. "I think I need to go home, dear. This is a lot to take in."

"Oh, of course." Mary sighed, and her shoulders drooped. She had hoped her friend would recognize her.

She walked Mrs. Garwood to the front door and waited as she put on her boots and coat.

"Goodbye, dear."

"Goodbye," Mary said. She watched as her friend walked back to her house. When Mrs. Garwood was safe inside, Mary closed the door.

THE FOLLOWING MORNING, Mary had just put some frozen waffles into the toaster when she heard the doorbell. She rushed to the door, hoping Mrs. Garwood had returned. She opened the door and saw her friend standing in her puffy coat.

"Please, come in," Mary said. "It's so nice to see you again."

Mrs. Garwood stepped into the entryway without any

greeting. Her face was still as pale as the day before, and her jaw was clenched.

After Mary closed the door, Mrs. Garwood looked her in the eyes. "If it's really you, Mary, then tell me. What's the name of my firstborn child?"

Mary's heart skipped a beat. She reached out and clasped her friend's hands. "Oh, Lydia. You don't have any children. You and Will tried for so long, getting poked and prodded for years. But it never happened."

Mary searched her friend's eyes for any hint of recognition. Then she continued, "You had Simon instead of Max, then. He was kind of like a furry kid. But he was never a substitute."

She embraced Mrs. Garwood. At first, her friend's muscles tightened. But then Mrs. Garwood relaxed as she hugged her.

"I suspect you have been like a mother to JoJo all these years. I am so grateful for that."

When they parted, the rose had returned to Mrs. Garwood's cheeks, and her mouth widened into a smile.

"Dear Mary? Can it really be you?" Mrs. Garwood stared at her. "I hadn't heard Anna called JoJo in years. Where have you been all this time?"

"Please take off your boots and coat and come in. I'll make some coffee, and we can talk."

<hr>

WHEN THEY WERE SEATED at the table with coffee in hand, Mary nodded toward the wall where the door had been. "That door appeared one morning after Jim went to work and JoJo got on the school bus. I was curious. I didn't mean to leave. I just wanted to see what was in there."

Mrs. Garwood sipped her coffee.

"I looked around for a little while. But when I was ready to come back, the door was gone."

"Oh, my . . . thirty years, dear. Thirty years." Mrs. Garwood said it quietly, like she was talking to herself.

"And then a couple of weeks ago, I saw the open doorway. I came back through the door and shut it. But—"

"Oh, it's so lovely that you're back, Mary dear. Anna is going to be so excited when she returns from her trip. She talks about you often."

"No, you don't understand."

"What is it, dear?"

"JoJo and Dustin aren't on vacation." She pointed at the wall. "They're in there."

Mrs. Garwood stared at her blankly.

"I didn't know it was her. I saw a woman and a man. But I couldn't fathom it was my little JoJo."

Mrs. Garwood put her head in her hands.

"I mean, look at me, Lydia. Do I look like I'm over sixty years old? Time works differently there. I had no idea it had been thirty years until I looked at a stupid yogurt cup." Mary squirmed. "I know it was wrong to shut the door even if it wasn't JoJo. It was a knee-jerk reaction."

Her friend was silent.

"Please say something. I can't stand the thought of you hating me."

Mrs. Garwood looked at Mary. "I'm trying to think it through, dear. It's a lot to process."

CHAPTER 18

Anna searched through the old desk for other clues from 1901. The lion heads on the front corners seemed to watch her every move. She knew it was her imagination. Yet, it unsettled her just the same.

She peered in the cubbyholes and pulled out the drawers. In one of the pigeonholes, she found a letter. A single name was written on the outside of the folded page:

Margaret

Anna looked up and saw Dustin walking toward her.

"Did you find anything else?" he asked.

She held up the folded page. "It looks like a letter. Should I open it?"

"I think it would be okay. Who would still be alive from 1901?"

Anna unfolded it and read:

My Dearest Maggie,

My heart is full of so many things I want to say to you. Each day, I think back on your every word, every gesture, every look. How foolish I was to go through that door. A life without you is an empty one. My heart breaks knowing you must think I left you. I hope one day this letter will find you—that my contemplations will somehow transfer from my mind to yours.

All my love,
Charles

"How sad," Anna said. "I wonder what happened to Chuck. Do you think he ever made it home?"

"I hope so."

Anna folded up the letter. When Dustin wasn't looking, she put it in her back pocket. "The letter is the only thing I found. All the other drawers are empty."

"Let's continue walking to confirm that it's a loop." Dustin rolled up his map in the parchment and tucked it under his arm.

"Just a minute." Anna walked to the table and grabbed the amethyst paperweight. "Okay, I'm ready."

***

THEY WALKED DOWN THE HALLWAY, away from the Big Kitchen. As they walked, the hallway widened. Before she knew it, she saw the music room ahead.

She hadn't noticed that the hallway narrowed when they walked the other way. But now, it was clear.

"You were right," she said. "There's the music room."

"Say again?"

"I said, you were right."

"One more time." Dustin grinned. He had heard her the first time.

"Ha. Ha. Ha." She mock-laughed at him.

They approached the music room and looked inside. "Will you play something while we're here?"

Dustin set the maps on the piano and sat on the bench. "What do you want me to play?"

"Whatever you want."

She relaxed in a chair and closed her eyes. Soon, she heard a lovely rendition of *Für Elise*. Lost in the music, she didn't want it to end. But then it did.

"That was beautiful," she said. "I wish the piano were closer to the Big Kitchen."

Dustin got up and examined the guitars. "We can't take the piano, but I can bring one of these." He settled on a Gibson and slung it on his back. "Maybe I can find some music in the library."

THEY CONTINUED their journey up the main hallway. As before, it seemed like it would never end. At some point, they stopped to rest and eat. Then, finally, they passed by the pool.

When they reached the library, Anna said, "I'm going to pop in and get another book. I'll meet you back in the Big Kitchen."

"Okay."

Anna pushed the ladder to a new place on the library's wall, one she hadn't looked at before, and climbed the rungs. She pulled out a book. *The Holy Bible*.

That was odd. There had been another Bible on a different shelf a few feet over. She put it back and chose another volume. *The Holy Bible.* She returned it. Her third choice was the same.

What was going on? As she pulled out Bible after Bible, she started throwing them on the floor. Before she knew it, she put her arm behind the remaining books on the shelf and shoved them down.

She looked at the pile of Bibles on the floor. On top, one lay open. It was tabbed, with notes in the margins and high-lighted passages. Even from a distance, she recognized it. It was her mom's.

"It's not fair, God." She flinched at the volume of her voice. "Why do we have to be trapped here? Why did you take my mom away from me?" As she descended the ladder, she missed a rung and fell. "Why?"

Anna felt the heat rise in her cheeks. She got up, pulled the amethyst paperweight out of her pocket, and hurled it at the window. She briefly heard the gratifying sound of glass break-ing. But then the window knit itself together.

She watched the dot of purple, now outside, arc and fall. There was a spark, a flicker, and, for a moment, a glimpse of stars hanging in space. Then the green hill returned, and the purple orb rolled across it to a stop. She stood wide-eyed as her mind tried to process what she had seen.

***

DUSTIN LEANED the Gibson guitar against the island in the Big Kitchen. As he spread out the maps, he caught movement from the corner of his eye. He looked up and saw a ball of fur zip by him.

He followed the movement down the main hallway. When he neared the library, he heard glass breaking. He rushed around the curve and saw Anna standing in the middle of the room, staring out the window.

ANNA JUMPED when she felt Dustin's hand on her shoulder.

"Are you okay?" he asked. "What's going on in here?"

"Did you see that?"

"See what?"

"The paperweight." She looked out the window again. The paperweight was by a patch of primrose.

"I was walking down the main hallway and thought I heard glass breaking." He furrowed his eyebrows.

"I threw the amethyst paperweight out the window."

"You what?"

"See the purple over there? That's it."

Anna turned. The pile of Bibles was gone. All but one of the books neatly lined the shelves again. On the end table by the recliner sat a single volume.

"I just came in here to get this," she said as she picked it up.

"And then you just happened to throw the paperweight at the window?"

Anna turned away. She didn't want him to see her face.

"Come on, Anna, you can talk to me."

"Do you really want to know?"

"Of course. I care about you."

Anna scrutinized his face. She wasn't sure if she should tell him about the flicker. Maybe she imagined it.

"Nothing makes sense. Why did my mom leave? And why are we trapped here? I feel like I'm going crazy. And I'm so tired. I'm just . . . *so* . . . tired."

Dustin put his arms around her and pulled her close.

"I'm not strong enough," she said. "I can't handle this."

CHAPTER 19

Mrs. Garwood sipped her coffee as Mary recounted what happened on the day she came back through the door. Mary told her how she walked up the smaller hallway and heard voices, how she hid from them, and how they walked down the larger hallway. She relayed how she saw the door, went through it, and shut it before she thought it through.

"Imagine how I felt when I realized it was JoJo, all grown up." Mary shook her head. "Oh, Lydia, I've lost so much time."

"It'll be okay, Mary. We'll figure it out together."

"I have so many questions about the things I've missed. But first, there's something I need to know."

"You can ask me anything, dear."

"Where's Jim? Did he remarry?"

Mrs. Garwood shifted in her chair and looked down at the table.

"What is it, Lydia?"

Mrs. Garwood looked up. "Oh, Mary dear. I don't know how to tell you."

"Tell me what?"

Mrs. Garwood looked down again and took a deep breath. Then she reached for Mary's hand. "About fourteen years ago," Mrs. Garwood said. "Oh my, has it been fourteen years?" She held Mary's hand tightly. "I guess there's no good way to say it, so I'll just get right to it. Jim was in a car accident, dear."

"Oh no, no . . ." A whimper escaped Mary's mouth.

"He didn't suffer. They said it was instantaneous. It was a head-on."

Mary sat with her mouth open and eyes wide as she processed the information. Jim was dead? It felt like a weight pressed on her chest. She squeezed her eyes shut. "No, that can't be," was all she could manage to say.

"I'm so sorry, dear."

Mary held fast to her friend's hand. Mrs. Garwood's voice grew distant and muffled. It sounded like it was at the bottom of a deep barrel. She tried to listen to her friend. But the thought that Jim was gone overwhelmed her mind. He was dead. She would never again see him, hear his voice, or feel his touch.

She grasped at her friend's words. If she could hold on to them, she could hear them. But she couldn't.

Her friend's voice faded further away. And then Mary fainted.

As Mary regained consciousness, she felt the hard boards beneath her. Something was poking her back. She struggled to reach it. When she opened her eyes, she saw Mrs. Garwood hovering over her. Her eyes were full of worry.

"Oh, Mary dear. Are you okay?"

"I just got dizzy."

"Here, take my hand."

"There's something on the floor under my back."

"Let's get you up first, and then we'll have a look."

Mrs. Garwood extended her hand. Mary took it, and Mrs. Garwood helped her up. When Mary was seated in the chair, Mrs. Garwood stooped and moved her hand over the floor. Then Mrs. Garwood picked up a small object. It was a key.

"Where did that come from?" Mary asked.

Mrs. Garwood handed her the key. It was large and tarnished—an antique key with a simple loop on one end and what looked like a small three-dimensional puzzle piece off the edge of the other.

"Maybe Anna or Dustin dropped it here and forgot about it?"

"Yeah, that's probably what happened." Mary put the key in her pocket. She stared at the wall and felt tears streaming down her cheeks. "Oh, Lydia. How did you bear it when Will passed away?"

Mrs. Garwood reached out and took Mary's hand. "It took a long time to get my bearings. And I still have difficult days."

Mary shook her head. "It can't be true. It just can't. How can he be gone?"

"I'm so sorry, Mary dear." Mrs. Garwood held her friend as she sobbed.

***

AFTER A WHILE, Mary pulled away and pressed a tissue against her eyes. "I'm feeling tired. I think I'm going to lie down. Lydia, would you stay here with me tonight? The other couch reclines."

"Of course, dear."

Mary went upstairs and returned with a pillow and blankets. As she set them on the couch, Mrs. Garwood said, "I'm going to go home and get something. I'll be back in a jiffy."

Before Mary could say anything, Mrs. Garwood put on her boots and puffy coat and went out the door. After several minutes, she returned with a small, rectangular metal case.

"What's that?" Mary asked.

"It's a laptop computer. Remember your computer with a big TV attached to a large box? This is like that, but so much more. I'll show you after you get a little rest."

"Wow, so many things are different now."

"They are indeed."

"I've been meaning to ask you. Where's the phone? The one that used to be in the kitchen isn't there anymore."

Mrs. Garwood pulled a small, rectangular object made of glass and metal from her pocket. "No one has a landline in their homes anymore, dear. We all carry a cell phone."

"I remember cell phones. But they were much larger than that."

"And now," Mrs. Garwood said, "we use them for just about everything but calling someone."

"I have so much to learn." Mary reached out and took her friend's hand. "Thanks for staying with me, Lydia. I don't know what I'd do without you."

"I'm just so glad you're back, Mary. Now, go lie down and try to rest."

CHAPTER 20

As they stepped out of the library, Anna saw a black kitten race past them toward the Big Kitchen. Then it turned around and stopped at Anna's feet.

Anna stooped and rubbed the kitten's ears. "Where did you come from?"

"I was following this little fur ball when I heard the glass breaking in the library."

Anna smiled. "Isn't he cute?" Then she saw his white feet and the white diamond patch on his chest. "Hey, this is Max, Mrs. Garwood's cat."

She looked at Dustin as they both said, "The door!"

Anna picked up Max, and they ran around the curve, by the Big Kitchen, and over to where the door should have been. Max jumped out of Anna's arms. He swatted at the wall. Then he arched his back and hissed.

"Even Max knows where the door should be," Dustin said.

"If he came through the door, then someone was able to see it and open it."

"Why would Mrs. Garwood come over to our house?"

Anna shrugged. "Do you think she knows we're in here?"

"I don't know."

Anna frowned. "I told you we should have been watching for the door."

"You didn't have to go with me. You could have stayed."

AFTER THEY ARGUED about missing the door, they agreed to resume taking turns watching for it. Dustin took the first watch. Meanwhile, Anna took her mom's Bible to the square bedroom.

Although she had been distracted by finding Max, her mental health was still precarious. One moment, everything didn't seem so bad. The next, she felt her mind slipping—to where, she couldn't be certain.

Anna sat on the bed and looked at the Bible. The outside was different; it was bound in the same leather as the other books in the library. But when she opened it, she recognized her mom's handwriting.

She moved her fingers over the indentations left from her mom's notes. Then she flipped through its pages. There were notes, highlights, and underlining on almost every page.

Anna closed it and held it close to her chest. And then the questions returned. "Why, God? Why didn't she come back?" She slumped over as sobs heaved from her chest.

She felt like she was falling into a deep, dark void—her mind barely hung on. She curled up into a fetal position. *Please help me, God. Please.* Over and over, she repeated the prayer until she fell asleep.

ANNA WOKE UP, still holding her mom's Bible. As the last vestiges of sleep fell away, she noticed her mind was more ordered. She felt like herself again. Nothing had changed;

their circumstances were the same. They were still trapped. All she had done was pray.

She sat up and opened the Bible. When she looked down, a verse caught her eye. The words were in red, so she knew it was something Jesus had said.

I am the door.

Anna knew the verse was talking about a person's salvation. Someone could only enter into a relationship with God the Father through His Son. Jesus made a way for everyone's sins to be forgiven. You had to go through the door, Jesus, to get to God the Father.

She had done that as a child. Her mom showed her how to pray. Yet, it was interesting to see the verse in light of their predicament.

She had turned her back on God when her mom disappeared. Maybe it was time to come back. She sat on the bed in the silence and looked up.

Dear God, if you can hear me, please help us get out of here.
Please forgive me for being mad at You. I want
to follow You. Please help us get back to our lives.
And please lead me to answers about my mom.

ANNA WALKED to the Big Kitchen and saw Dustin sitting at the island. Both maps were open, side-by-side. Max sat on the edge of the map, watching Dustin trace one of the lines on Charles's map with his finger.

As Dustin's finger slid across the paper, Max pounced on Dustin's hand. Then Max rolled over on his back and flipped onto his feet. He batted Dustin's hand a few times and lay down in the middle of the map.

Anna laughed. Dustin rubbed Max's ears.

"He's kind of like a ninja kitty," Anna said. She picked Max up and held him close. "Did you find anything?"

"I think so," Dustin said. "Check this out." He pointed at Charles's map. "This is where the Big Kitchen is. And here's our door."

"Our door?" Anna never heard him say *our* door before. It was always *the* door.

"Now, look down here on this smaller hallway. It shows a second door here." Dustin pointed at the notation of a door that corresponded with a number on a hallway they hadn't been down.

"And here's a third door on this one." Sure enough, there was another reference to a door.

"There are other doors?" The way Anna said it sounded like both a statement and a question.

"That's what the map shows."

"Do you think they lead to other houses?"

Dustin shrugged. "Maybe."

Anna sat beside him, and Max jumped onto the floor.

"That makes me think of a dream I had," Anna said. "Actually, I don't know if it was a dream or a memory."

"What happened?"

"I was sitting at the kitchen table with my dad, eating breakfast. Well, he wasn't eating—I was. He was reading a newspaper. I looked up and saw the door. I got up and went over to it. As I reached out and felt the doorknob, I said, 'Hey, Dad. Look at this door. Where did it come from?' And he said, 'Stop playing around. Finish eating your breakfast so you're not late for school.'"

"How old were you?"

"Maybe eight or nine?"

"What do you think it means?"

"I don't know." Anna sighed.

"If it was a memory," Dustin said, "do you think that means your mom found the door? Could she be here?"

A smile spread over Anna's face. "You know, I think she could be." Why hadn't she thought of that? Her mom could be here, *somewhere*.

"Maybe we should look for her," he said.

"But what if the door opens again——" Anna's eyes narrowed and then grew wide. "If it's a memory and my mom is here, then I could've opened the door and let her out. It's my fault."

"It's not your fault." Dustin put his arms around her. She put her head on his chest as he embraced her. "How could you have known?"

"It feels like it's my fault. Why didn't I open the door?"

Max rubbed his neck on Anna's leg and purred.

"See," Dustin said, "even Max agrees with me."

Anna pulled away. "What if we go look for my mom and the door comes back while we're gone?"

"If it means finding her, that's a chance we'll have to take."

CHAPTER 21

Mary and Mrs. Garwood were sitting on the couch the next morning when the doorbell rang. Mary looked at Mrs. Garwood and motioned for her to follow. Then she went to the den and peeked out of the shutter.

"It's a police officer," Mary whispered. "What should we do?"

"Go upstairs, and I'll take care of it."

Mary hurried up the steps and into the loft. The doorbell rang a second time. Mary sat on the floor by the bookcase. The sound of the door opening funneled up into the loft.

"Good morning, ma'am. I'm Officer Springer with the Littleton Police Department."

"Good morning, officer. I'm Lydia Garwood."

"Is Dustin Hughes home?"

"No, dear, he's on vacation. Can I help you with something?"

"We received a call from his employer. He missed a tax court hearing, and no one's heard from him. They said he's never missed a hearing before."

"Oh my, I'm sure he hasn't. But everyone makes a mistake at some point. It must have slipped his mind."

"When was the last time you saw him?"

"Before I get to that, please come in, just inside the door. It's freezing out there. I can see your breath. You'll catch a cold being out there so long."

"I've been in worse. But thank you. I appreciate it."

Mary cringed. Why did she invite him in? She heard his footsteps and the door as it closed.

"What was your question?" Mrs. Garwood said.

"I asked when you last saw him."

"Oh, yes. A few weeks ago, before they left. He came over and helped me get a box out of the basement."

"He came over? To where?"

"To my house. I live next door. Over that way."

Mary pictured Mrs. Garwood pointing.

"His employer said he's married to a . . ." Mary heard him flip through the pages of a notepad. "Anna?"

"Yes, dear."

"Is Anna with him?"

"Yes, but I don't know where they went or when they'll return. I'm sure I'll hear all about it when they get back."

"What are you doing here?"

"I came over to check on things while they're gone."

"I'm okay," Officer Springer said.

"What's that?"

"I was talking to dispatch and letting them know I'm alright."

As she listened to them talking, Mary shifted and pulled her leg out from under her. Her calf was numb, and she hoped moving it would wake it up.

"How long have you known them?" Officer Springer asked.

"Oh my, let me think. I've known Anna since she was a

wee one. You know, she lived in this house while she was growing up. I was friends with her mom, Mary."

"Do you mind if I look around?"

Mary held her breath. *Say no, please say no.*

"Oh, I wouldn't feel comfortable with that—it not being my house and all."

"Okay, that's fine. But I'll need to check your identification."

"Of course. But I don't have it with me, dear. My purse is at home. Could you follow me over to my house?"

"Sure, no problem."

Mary heard Mrs. Garwood putting on her boots. "Okay, officer, I'm ready."

After Mary heard them walk outside and the key turn in the lock, she breathed in deeply and let it out slowly. She sprang up to look out of the shutter in the loft, but her calf was still numb. She winced from the pins and needles and limped to the window.

Looking out, she saw Officer Springer following Mrs. Garwood up the steps to her front porch. She started to leave the loft but decided it would be better to wait—just in case he came back.

Mary sat by the bookcase, rubbing her calf. The pins and needles subsided. She looked through Anna's collection of books. There were titles by Jane Austen, John Steinbeck, and Emily Brontë. And then it caught her eye—her Bible. She pulled it off the shelf and flipped through it. She ran her fingers over the pages and noticed a verse she had highlighted.

So I will restore to you the years that
the swarming locust has eaten,
the crawling locust, the consuming locust,
and the chewing locust.

Beside the verse, she had written a note:

God can restore our years of unfruitfulness and somehow make up for lost time.

She closed the Bible. She had once believed it. But could God actually do that? Her faith was weak. But she didn't know how to make it strong again.

MARY WAS LOST in her thoughts when she heard the key in the lock. She froze and waited to see if Mrs. Garwood was alone. Then she heard her friend call to her.

"It's just me, dear. You can come down now."

Mary jumped up and hurried down the stairs. "Is everything okay?"

"Oh, yes. I saw him go over to Mr. Hagestrom's house. I watched from my window. I guess he wanted to check out my story. When he came out of Mr. Hagestrom's house, he got into his patrol car and left."

"Do you think he'll come back?"

"I don't know. He gave me his card and told me to call if I heard from them. He said he just wants to be sure they're alright."

"I didn't know you had a key."

"Anna gave it to me years ago. It's handy when you lock yourself out or have a package that needs putting in from the porch. I don't use it much. I wouldn't barge in on them."

Mary smiled. "Of course, Lydia. I didn't think you would. There are others, on the other hand—"

"Are you talking about Martha?"

"Yes, I've encountered Dustin's mom. Let's just say I don't think she's too happy with me. I told her I'm housesitting."

"Martha's a good woman. She's just had a hard time as a mom letting go of her son."

CHAPTER 22

Anna watched Dustin examine the map.

"The closest door is in the small hallway that goes by the music room," he said.

Anna nodded. "Do you want to head that way?"

"Sure."

Dustin rolled up the maps, and they started down the main hallway. As they walked, Anna periodically called out for her mom.

"Do you think you should call out her name instead?" Dustin asked.

"You're right. Mary might get her attention better."

Besides calling out now and again, they walked in silence. Max walked with them, occasionally doing his part by meowing loudly.

After a while, they smelled breakfast and stopped to eat the croissants and scrambled eggs. Small bowls with food and water were on the floor beside the table for Max. Anna's stomach roiled, but she ate anyway.

As soon as they finished, they continued down the main hallway. It felt like they would never get there. Anna was tired, but she pushed on. When they reached the music room, they turned left.

"Now that we're closer," Dustin said, "let's look at the map again." He unfurled Charles's map on a nearby table. "The door should be about halfway down this hallway in a small kitchen."

"How do you know it's a small kitchen?"

"That's how it's labeled."

Anna looked where Dustin pointed. Sure enough, the calligraphic writing on the map's key said, *Small Kitchen*.

"How will we know when we're halfway?" Anna asked.

"Right before that, there's a greenhouse."

"That sounds interesting."

They continued walking and calling out to her mom. They passed by bedrooms, sitting rooms, and a den. The rooms seemed to blend together.

After it felt like they had been walking for hours, Max dashed out in front of them. Anna called out to him and started to run. But she was tired and slowed her pace back to a walk.

Before long, Max sprinted back and ran in circles around them as if trying to tell them he had found something. When Anna looked up, she saw a glass-enclosed room on the left. Although the pool room was also enclosed in glass, this room looked different.

Dustin opened the door. He held it open for Anna, and she stepped through.

Inside were a variety of exotic-looking plants. On one side, Anna saw bougainvillea and jasmine. There were different types of vines and hibiscus. Various shades of red, orange, yellow, and green overwhelmed her senses.

She tipped her head back. The ceiling was also made of glass. A soft light filtered through the plants. As Anna looked around the room, she spotted finches and robins. She heard water, like a gushing stream, coming from somewhere in the back.

Max frolicked around the room. When he stopped for a moment, a butterfly landed on his nose. And then he was off again, chasing after the butterfly as it flitted back and forth, just out of his reach.

"Let's find the water," Anna said.

Dustin followed her down a narrow stone path. As they walked, the sound of rushing water grew louder. And soon, she saw a small pond with a fountain. Lilies floated in the water.

"This looks amazing."

By the path was a bench where you could watch the fountain. Dustin and Anna sat, and Anna stared up at the glass ceiling.

"What are you doing?" Dustin asked.

"I'm looking for the sun. It's always daytime, but I've never seen the sun here."

"I don't see it either."

"What would it look like if we could see the stars from this room?" Anna said. She thought about the flicker and wondered if she should tell Dustin about it.

"It never gets dark," he said. "So, how could we see stars? Let's keep looking for your mom."

Anna looked at the pale blue sky for another moment, and then she followed Dustin out of the room.

As they entered the Small Kitchen, Anna surveyed the room.

Dustin looked down at the map. "The map says the door should be beside an icebox."

"What's an icebox?"

"I think it's like a refrigerator," he said.

"What does it look like?"

"I'm not sure."

Anna pointed. "Look at that wooden box. It looks like a cabinet, but it doesn't match the rest of the décor in here."

The oak cabinet stood about four feet high with three doors on the front: a longer door on the left and two smaller doors on the right. The top right door was medium-sized, and the door on the bottom right was the smallest. Each door had brass hinges toward the outside of the cabinet, indicating that they all opened outward.

Dustin swung the small, metal arm on the brass latch of the left door outward and pulled it open. On the inside, the door was lined with tin. A metal tray toward the top held a block of ice.

"I'm guessing this is the icebox," Anna said.

"Yeah, it's super cool."

Anna giggled.

"I can't believe you laughed at that one," Dustin said. He opened the right side of the icebox. In it, metal shelves were filled with fresh fruit, vegetables, and meat.

A few feet to the left of the icebox was a four-panel mahogany door. The door was about seven feet high. A brass doorknob with an intricate floral pattern stood out against the dark wood. And below the brass knob was a keyhole.

Max ran over and batted at the door, arched his back, and hissed—just like he had batted the wall where the door should have been in the Big Kitchen.

Beside the door, Vincent van Gogh's *The Road to Saint-Remy* hung by a chair. His post-impressionist palette-knife strokes made it look like a dream. An indistinct woman walked toward her like she was coming to greet her.

Anna twisted the doorknob, but it didn't move. She pushed on the door to no avail. "It must be locked."

"Where do you think the door goes?" Dustin said.

"Maybe it goes to Paris. I've always wanted to go there."

Dustin smiled at her. "Cheaper travel but terribly unreliable."

Anna laughed. But then she frowned. "Do you think my mom could have gone through a different door?"

Her question was rhetorical. Still, he said, "I think anything is possible."

Anna looked at her feet. A tear had rolled out of the corner of her eye, and she didn't want him to see it. What if her mom had gone through a different door? Her thought was interrupted by the smell of food.

"Do you smell that?" Anna asked.

"Is it time for lunch already?"

When she looked over, a spread of sumptuous-looking foods arrayed the table. A small bowl of applesauce sat beside a platter of roast pork. Other bowls held mashed potatoes, creamed cabbage, green corn, and pickled beets. On the side, there was a peach cake with whipped cream, small plates of cheese and wafers, and a light yellow, enameled coffee pot with a large spout.

"This looks more like dinner than lunch," Anna said.

"I remember reading that people in the early 1900s ate a larger meal at lunchtime and a smaller one at dinnertime."

"The beets and cabbage look weird."

"I'm guessing they ate those dishes back then."

"Yeah, you're probably right." The roast pork smelled good, but she wasn't hungry. She felt nauseated. She poured them coffee and stirred several lumps of sugar into her cup. Dustin drank his black.

When Dustin put his fork to his mouth, Anna said, "Wait—"

"Why?"

"I think we should give thanks. I remember how my mom used to do it."

"Good idea. Go ahead."

After she thanked God for the food, she forced herself to

eat so Dustin wouldn't worry. When they finished, they took their coffee cups to a nearby sitting room with a large table. Dustin spread out the map, and Max jumped into Anna's lap. He purred when Anna hugged him.

As Dustin looked at the map, Anna smelled cookies. She turned and saw them on the end table. She picked up the plate and held it near Dustin's arm.

"Do you want a cookie?"

Dustin grabbed one and kept searching the map for the third door. "I thought it was right here," he mumbled.

Anna bit into a cookie as she leaned over to look. "Here it is." She pointed at another smaller hallway that was closer to where the main hallway circled around at the bottom of the map.

"Okay, let's go back to the main hallway, and we'll regroup."

CHAPTER 23

Mary perused the contents of the refrigerator. "Maybe I could make us some macaroni and cheese? There's a brick of cheddar and some noodles in the pantry."

Mrs. Garwood pressed her lips together. "Mary dear, you're almost out of groceries."

"Yeah, it's getting sparse. But I don't know how to get more. I don't have any money."

"Oh, don't worry about that," Mrs. Garwood said. "I can buy them. And we can order them online."

"Online? What's that?"

"Oh, I forgot. So much has changed since you left. There's a website for everything now."

"Website?"

"Come sit down, and I'll show you."

Mrs. Garwood opened her laptop. Mary watched as her friend moved her finger on a square inset in the metal, which moved the cursor around on the screen. The cursor looked like the one on Jim's computer. The monitor had been like a TV, and they had moved the cursor around with a mouse.

When Mrs. Garwood tapped on the metal, a window opened on the screen. "This is a browser."

Mary watched her friend type something in the browser. Then, the browser changed, and the name of the grocery store she used to go to was displayed on the screen. Before she knew it, they had ordered milk, eggs, fruit, vegetables, and other things.

"It should be delivered on the porch around 2:00," Mrs. Garwood said. "You won't even have to answer the front door."

"Thank you, Lydia. You're the best."

"No problem, dear. It's nice to be needed. When you get this old, nobody needs you much anymore."

"What else is online?" Mary asked.

"Oh, all sorts of things. News. Stores. Movies. You name it, it's there."

Mary inhaled and breathed out slowly as she tapped her fingers on the table. "Could I look up an article about Jim?"

Mrs. Garwood opened her mouth and paused. "Are you sure you want to do that?"

"No, but I would like to know more about what happened."

Mrs. Garwood typed in Jim's name and the date of the accident. When the results came up, she moved her laptop closer to Mary. "Here you go. Just put the cursor on the one you want to open and press down on the mouse pad."

Mary moved her finger around on the square and positioned the cursor over something from *The Littleton Daily News,* the newspaper that used to be delivered to her front porch. She took a deep breath and pressed on the metal. A new page opened with an article titled *Local Man Dead at 48.* It was dated May 19, 2007, and included a picture of Jim.

She stared at Jim's photo. He looked distinguished with gray in the temples of his hair. She missed him so much. Her heart seemed to swell inside her chest, and she had trouble breathing deeply.

"I guess this doesn't matter. But did he ever get involved with someone else?"

"No, Mary dear. I don't think he even went on a date."

"I'm not sure I can read it. Would you read it to me?"

"Of course, dear."

Mary pushed the laptop in front of Mrs. Garwood, and Mrs. Garwood read it out loud.

James "Jim" Bauer died last night after being hit head-on by a drunk driver traveling down the wrong side of the highway. "It's tragic and senseless," Officer Springer said. "The accident could have been easily avoided if the man had taken a cab instead of driving while intoxicated."

"Oh my, look at that, Mary. I wonder if it's the same officer who came here."

Mary looked at the screen where Mrs. Garwood pointed. "That's interesting. I suppose it could be."

Mrs. Garwood continued reading.

Mr. Bauer was a beloved member of the community. He was survived by his daughter, Anna, and his son-in-law, Dustin. His wife, Mary, went missing in 1991 and was never found.

Mary's eyes widened, and she looked down at her hands. "Lydia, would you tell me what happened here the day I went through the door?"

"Oh, Mary. I don't think you need to dredge all that up. What good would it do?"

"Maybe it would give us a clue about how to get Anna and Dustin back."

"Are you sure?"

"Yes, Lydia. I'll be okay."

Mrs. Garwood shifted in her seat and cleared her throat. "That afternoon, I called you. Someone picked up, but they didn't say anything. And then they hung up the phone."

"That's odd."

"A little while later, Anna came to my house. She was scared and didn't want to go home by herself."

"Why was she afraid?"

"Now let me think. It's been a long time." Mrs. Garwood grimaced.

"It's okay, Lydia. Take your time."

"Oh, yes. Now I remember. She said she saw a man run out of her house. When we got here, the door wasn't shut all the way."

"That doesn't make sense. I would have never left the door open. What did you do?"

"We looked all over the house for you. When I couldn't find you, I called Jim, and he came home early."

"Anna said a man ran out of the house? Are you sure?"

Mrs. Garwood nodded.

Mary tilted her head and rubbed her neck. A man had run out of the house. "Did she describe him?"

"I don't think so. But I don't remember."

Mary stared into the distance. Who was he? And then it hit her.

"Maybe he was in there." She pointed at the wall. "And when he ran out, he closed the door like I did."

CHAPTER 24

Anna and Dustin walked toward the main hallway. When they passed by the greenhouse, Max circled them and darted over to its door. Clearly, he wanted to explore the room again. Yet, as they kept walking, he followed them.

They continued calling out for Anna's mom. When they reached the main hallway, Dustin sat at a table and spread out the maps. Anna sat beside him and looked around the small room. On the wall by the table was a panel with buttons and knobs.

She got up and pressed one of the buttons. A light came on over the table. She pushed it again, and it turned off. She pressed another button and heard something lurch. She pressed and held the button and heard a whirring sound.

Dustin pointed to the ceiling. "Look."

She looked up and saw the ceiling moving like a sunroof in a car. As it receded, it revealed a layer of glass. Anna continued holding the button until it stopped. The pale blue sky covered them, and a soft light filled the room.

Anna smiled. She left it open and sat. Max jumped into her lap.

She leaned over to look at the maps. Then she heard a soft *tink*—the sound a small rock makes when it hits the car's windshield while you're driving. She looked at the glass ceiling. There was a small black rock on the glass.

As she watched, a few more pebbles hit the glass. They plinked, bounced, and came to rest above them.

Then a mixture of pebbles and larger rocks rained down on the glass. The sound was deafening, and the glass splintered from the force of the larger ones. A split second after each crack, the glass knit itself back together.

They stared at the sight wide-eyed with their mouths open. Max shook and tried to climb under Anna's arm.

And then a baseball-sized rock smashed through the glass. The rock went through the table, leaving a large hole. The glass momentarily shattered with shards suspended in mid-air. But like a movie playing in reverse, the pieces quickly moved back together.

The glass was restored in the blink of an eye. Yet, for an instant, Anna saw the pale blue sky flicker. In that moment, it was filled with a breathtaking display of stars.

As quickly as the hailstorm of rocks began, it finished. A soft light filtered through the skylight and cast diffused, almost indistinguishable, shadows of the stones onto the table. Max pressed close to Anna.

"Did you see that?" Anna asked.

"What was that?"

"I don't know. But didn't it look awesome?"

Dustin got up. He pushed and held the button. As the ceiling panel whirred back into place, Anna watched until the pale blue sky disappeared.

After it was closed, Dustin sat on the chair. "Maybe that's why there aren't any doors that lead outside."

"Or windows that open," Anna added.

Anna looked down at the table. The hole in it was already

gone. She leaned under the table and picked up the rock. It was black, shiny, and heavy with small holes.

She handed it to Dustin. "I think it's a meteorite."

"Yeah, it looks like a stony-iron."

"A what?"

"A stony-iron. You know, a type of meteorite."

"How do you know that?"

"Didn't you take astronomy in college?"

"You're just a show-off." Anna smiled at him and stuck out her tongue.

Dustin laughed. "Seriously, though, we need to find your mom and a way out of here." He looked at the map and pointed. "The third door is here. If we go down the main hallway a little further, we'll turn left on the path by the Grey Room."

"What does that mean?"

"I don't know," Dustin said. "Maybe it's painted grey?"

"I don't remember seeing a grey room before."

"Me either. But if we see the path narrow or the weird desk, we'll know we've gone too far."

Dustin rolled up the maps and got up. Anna stood with Max in her arms and followed him.

***

THEY WALKED down the main hallway in silence. Anna was thinking about the stony-iron. What if other meteorites made it through the ceiling? She wondered if Dustin was thinking about it too.

Soon, she saw another hallway on their left. Sure enough, a room on their right was painted in various shades of grey. Anna looked into the room. The couch and chairs were upholstered in a light-grey, floral pattern. White fluffy pillows were displayed neatly on either end of the couch. But when she looked out the window, the hills were still green, and the wildflowers were shades of pink, yellow, and purple.

Anna plopped down on the couch. "Should we look at Charles's map again?"

Dustin sat beside her and opened the map on the bluish-grey wood. "Doesn't this look like beetle-kill pine? Remember, we saw a table made from it at the home and garden show last year."

"Oh yeah, I remember. It does look like that."

Max jumped on the couch between them and leaned forward like he was looking at the map. When Dustin put his finger on the map, Max leaped onto Dustin's hand, lost his footing, and slid off the table. Anna laughed. Then Max ran around the table and jumped into Anna's lap.

"The third door is also by a kitchen. But this one's not as far down the hallway."

Anna rested her head on one of the pillows. "This pillow is as soft as it looks."

"Are you ready to go?"

"Not yet. Can we rest for a minute?"

"Sure."

"What if we don't find her?" she asked.

"I think we'll find her."

"How do you know?"

"It's just a feeling." Dustin reached over and took Anna's hand in his.

CHAPTER 25

When they woke up the next morning, Mary looked at Mrs. Garwood. "We need a plan, Lydia. I feel so helpless. We need to come up with something."

"Well, dear, let's start with what you know. Then maybe we can come up with a plan."

"That's a good way of looking at it."

"What do you know about the door?" Mrs. Garwood asked.

"It seems to show up on Mondays. Anyway, I think it does. I was a little fuzzy on the days of the week when I came back through the door. But it was Monday when I went through it the first time, and it was Monday when you saw it."

"That's something. It's Thursday. So that gives us a few days. What else do you know?"

"If you don't go through it when it opens and you try to leave it open to watch, it'll close by itself. That happened twice."

"Okay, anything else?"

"It's the only way I know to get to Anna and Dustin." Mary's fingers moved over the table as she thought. Feeling the nuances in the wood's texture helped her to focus. Then her muscles tightened as she looked straight into her friend's eyes. "I know what I have to do. If the door comes back, I'm going through it to look for JoJo."

"Oh, Mary. There must be some other way."

"I let JoJo down so many years ago, and I'm not going to let her down now."

Mrs. Garwood frowned. "I don't want to lose you again. But I don't see another way either."

"Promise me, Lydia, that you'll do whatever you can to keep the door open."

"You have my word."

The two friends hugged.

"Thanks, Lydia. It has meant a lot having you here with me."

"What are we going to do until Monday?" Mrs. Garwood asked. "Do you want to play cribbage?"

"I have an idea. You'll never guess what I found. I'll be right back." Mary hurried down the basement stairs and returned with an armful of photo albums.

Over the next few days, the two friends looked through the old photos and reminisced. Mary found a cribbage board in the den, and they had a tournament. They ate good food, talked, laughed, and cried. By Monday, it felt as if they had never been apart.

ON MONDAY MORNING, Mary pulled a pan out of the drawer beneath the stove. "How would you like your egg, Lydia?"

"Over easy, just enough to cook the white."

Mary cracked an egg into the buttered pan. Bacon popped and crackled on another burner, filling the room with its aroma. When it was finished, Mary brought their plates to the table.

"You cooked. I'll give thanks." Mrs. Garwood prayed.

As Mary took her first bite, the doorbell rang.

"I'll see who it is," Mrs. Garwood said.

"Okay, I'll stay here and keep an eye out for the door."

Mary listened to her friend's steps as she walked to the front door. When the door opened, she heard Mrs. Garwood say, "Officer Springer. What brings you back here this morning?"

Mary shifted in her seat. What was *he* doing here?

"Good morning, Mrs. Garwood. I see you're here early, checking on things. Are you cooking bacon?"

"Oh, yes. My stove wasn't working. I knew Anna and Dustin wouldn't mind. Can I help you with something?"

"Can you believe it snowed again last night? It's not quite an inch. But I don't recall ever getting so much snow."

Mary wondered if he had noticed there weren't any footprints.

"I don't remember either, dear."

"We received another call. This time, it was from Dustin's mom. She hadn't heard from her son and was worried about him. Have you heard anything from them?"

"Not yet. But I imagine they'll be back any day now."

"She also said she came by and saw a woman staying here. The woman claimed she was housesitting."

"Martha's a bit nosy and overprotective. Her son is in his thirties, but you wouldn't know that by the way she acts. She hasn't been able to let go."

"Even if that's true, I still need to follow up on her call. Have you seen a woman staying here?"

Mary's stomach dropped. But then she looked up and saw it. "The door's back," she shouted. "Come quick, Lydia, and make sure it stays open."

Mary rushed to the door, pushed down on the bronze lever, and opened it wide. As she stepped through, the quiet enveloped her. She looked around but didn't see Anna or Dustin.

Then she looked back through the door at the kitchen and saw Mrs. Garwood rush in and stop in front of the door. Officer Springer followed. She watched Officer Springer gesture as he spoke. She imagined he was asking who had said that and where she had gone. In response, Mrs. Garwood pointed at her on the other side of the open door.

When Officer Springer looked in her direction, it was obvious he couldn't see her or the door. He looked straight at her without any hint of recognition.

But when Mrs. Garwood looked her way, Mary waved to her friend. Her friend smiled and waved back. Then Mary looked to her left at the Big Kitchen and ran down the main hallway.

Mrs. Garwood stood in front of the open door. "Would you be a dear and get me one of those chairs?"

Officer Springer picked up a chair and set it beside Mrs. Garwood.

"Thank you, dear." Mrs. Garwood positioned the chair against the open door and sat on it.

"What are you doing?" Officer Springer asked.

"I'm making sure the door doesn't close."

"What door?"

"The one behind me."

"I don't see a door." Officer Springer frowned. "Are you feeling okay, ma'am?"

"Never better." Mrs. Garwood looked at him and smiled.

Officer Springer walked toward her. "And where exactly is this door?"

She pointed. "The doorway is right there."

Mrs. Garwood watched Officer Springer pat the open doorway like it was a wall.

"Oh my, you can't see it, can you?" She turned in the chair. "Here, let me show you." She leaned forward and reached through the doorway with her hand.

Officer Springer jerked backward, and his eyebrows lifted. "What happened to your hand?"

Mrs. Garwood laughed and pulled it back. "Don't worry, dear. It's right here."

"But it was gone for a moment. What kind of trick is that?"

"Come here and give me your hand."

Officer Springer tilted his head and frowned.

"It's okay," she said. "I'm not going to try anything funny. I have an idea I want to try." She took his hand and pulled it through the open doorway and back.

Officer Springer gasped.

"See, there's an open doorway. And I need to make sure the door doesn't close."

He shook his head. Then he reached over and keyed up his mic. "I'm okay."

"You don't look okay."

"I was talking to dispatch."

"Oh."

"It doesn't make any sense," Officer Springer said.

"I know." Mrs. Garwood looked at the clock on the microwave. It was 11:11. "But you might as well sit down. It's going to be a while."

CHAPTER 26

Anna and Dustin stood in a small kitchen. Beside the kitchen was the third door. The door wasn't like the other doors. It was smaller with a small brass knob instead of a bronze lever.

Next to the door, a painting hung on the wall: *The Road Home* by Walter Withers. A solitary figure stood on the path. A summer day, a stroll down the lane. In the background, a suggestion of a house. Would the woman return home?

Anna turned the knob and pushed the door open a crack. Then, a few inches. She peered through at a kitchen.

"What do you see?"

"Not much yet. It looks like no one is home." Anna looked back at Dustin. "Where's Max?"

"He's right here."

"Maybe you should hold him so he doesn't run through."

Dustin reached down and picked Max up. "I've got him."

Anna opened the door a little wider. She heard her breath catch as anxiety crept through her chest and into her stomach. It was her kitchen. To be more exact, it was her mother's kitchen.

The red phone hung on the wall, its long cord almost

touching the floor. She remembered how her mom would prop the handset between her ear and shoulder so she could talk to someone as she walked around the kitchen preparing dinner.

She used to call her friend Sarah on that phone. She would stretch its cord around the corner and down the hallway where she sat on the floor with her back against the wall, whispering secrets. For a moment, she wondered what had happened to Sarah.

A large wall clock, black and circular, hung by the table. It was 3:15. If it were a weekday, her dad would likely be at work. And she wouldn't be home from school yet.

"What is it?" Dustin asked. "Anna, what's wrong?"

She swung the door open so Dustin could see. "Look, it's our kitchen. But it's from when I was a kid."

Anna looked at Dustin. She could tell he was processing the new information. He had that look he got when he was assessing risk.

Max wiggled as he tried to escape from Dustin's arms. She turned back to look through the door. Before she knew it, she was stepping over the threshold.

"Wait!" Dustin grabbed her arm to hold her back. When he did, Max jumped out of his arms and bolted through the door.

Anna called Max's name and ran after him. Dustin put his hand to his head, sighed, and followed her.

As Anna went through the door, she saw Max bounding down the hallway. He turned and ran up the stairs. She stood and listened to the ambiance. She heard a hum from the refrigerator. An airplane flew overhead. And then the phone rang. She instinctively grabbed the handset and put it to her ear.

"Hello?" the caller asked. "Is anyone there?" And, "Mary? Mary dear, is that you? Are you home?"

Anna quickly hung up the phone. She knew the voice. When she turned, she saw Dustin standing just inside the door.

"That was Mrs. Garwood," she said.

Anna scanned the room. There were her mom's keys on the hook. There, her mom's shoes on the shoe shelf. And her mom's purse sat on the counter. Anna opened the door to the garage. Her mom's car was parked inside.

Beside the phone hung a calendar with big, block numerals reminding everyone that it was 1991. Some of the days on the calendar were crossed off. That had been her idea, a way to keep track of the time.

It was October 14, 1991. Anna pointed at the calendar. "October 14 is the day my mom disappeared. Do you think we could have gone back in time?" There was a glint of hope in her voice, hope mixed with despair because it looked like her mom had already gone through the door. "Why would it bring us back to when my mom had already left?"

Dustin shook his head.

"I won't come home until about 3:30," Anna said. "So I have time to look for Max." It was weird talking about the past in present terms.

She started toward the stairs but noticed Dustin wasn't walking with her. She turned and saw him standing by the door. "Aren't you coming?"

"I'm going to keep an eye on the door. If it starts to close and I can't keep it from closing, I'll squeeze back through. I can see this door, so I could open it again for you."

"Good idea."

Anna turned back toward the stairs. She meant to hurry, but nostalgia overtook her.

There was a wall between the kitchen and the living room. When she passed the living room doorway, she saw the oak entertainment center against the wall with the small tube TV in the middle. Its cabinet doors hid books and random supplies. The shelves displayed nicer-looking books and porcelain figurines.

She opened one of the cubbies and saw the *Narnia* series by C.S. Lewis. Her parents had read them to her. She pulled one of the books out and turned it over in her hands. She loved that series. She remembered pretending she was Lucy each time.

She put the book away, shut the cabinet door, and walked down the hallway. The front door was ajar; she had forgotten that detail. She was glad Max went upstairs instead of out the front door.

She climbed the stairs and found Max sitting on the bed in her room. "There you are," she said as she picked him up. She rubbed his ears. "We don't want you getting stuck in 1991. Although you'd probably like Simon."

She looked at the plastic stars on the ceiling. Should she leave herself a note? No, it would be better not to mess with anything.

A fleeting thought went through her head. Could Charles have been the man she saw dart out the front door? And then she heard a little voice shout, "Mom!" and small feet running down the hallway toward the kitchen.

Anna crept down the stairs, avoiding the squeaky step. Her younger self was calling out and searching the kitchen. She heard the door to the garage open and close. When she heard the back door open, she hurried down the hallway and saw Mrs. Garwood step outside.

Anna ran to the kitchen. She looked to her right. Mrs. Garwood stood on the back porch, looking toward the oak tree. Dustin held the door open a crack. She pushed through it and closed the door behind her.

"That was a close one," Anna said. "Good call on waiting by the door."

She watched the door and waited for it to disappear into the wall. It didn't. The door remained visible with its brass knob contrasting with the bronze in the room and *The Road Home* hanging beside it. The woman in the painting seemed to ponder whether she would turn around or continue walking away from her home toward a new adventure.

As Anna started to say something, the floor quaked. She fell forward, but Dustin caught her. And then everything was still.

CHAPTER 27

As Mary ran by the library, the floor shook. She lost her footing, hit the wall, and fell.

She looked up and gasped. For a moment, the rolling green hills disappeared from the window. In their place were stars. She squeezed her eyes closed. When she opened them, the green hills were back, covered by wildflowers under the pale blue sky.

The shaking stopped. She had never been in an earthquake, but she imagined that was how it would feel—like turbulence on an airplane.

Mary stood and listened for what might have caused it. When she didn't hear or see anything, she took a few steps. For the moment, the shaking didn't resume.

Anna stared at the wall.

"Are you okay?" Dustin asked.

"What do you think happened?"

Max jumped out of Anna's arms, walked to the door, and sat by it.

"Maybe it was a bigger stony-iron?"

"I think we might be running out of time," Anna said.

"What did you see in there?"

"The front door was open just like it had been that day. But I didn't see the man."

"So, maybe he'd already left?"

"He must have."

"Do you think the man was Charles?" Dustin asked.

"That's exactly what I was thinking."

Max continued sitting by the door, looking at Anna, as if trying to tell her something.

Anna pointed to the door. "Do you see that? Why is it still there?" She walked to the door and held the brass knob in her hand. "Hold Max so he doesn't run through the door again."

Dustin picked Max up and held him. Anna opened the door a crack and peered through. She didn't see anyone. By now, her smaller self should be standing in the kitchen while Mrs. Garwood talked to her dad on the phone. Yet, the room was empty.

She opened the door a few inches, then a few more, so she could see the clock.

"It's 3:15 again," Anna said. "I think it's on some sort of time loop."

Anna waited, watching the minutes pass. When it was 3:30, she saw young Anna burst through the front door and down the hallway toward her.

She closed the door, stepped back, and observed the door. After a few minutes, the door was still there.

"Open it and see if the time rolls back again," Dustin said. Max purred as Dustin rubbed his ears.

Anna turned the brass knob and opened the door just enough to see through it. No one was there. Then she opened it enough to see the clock. It was 3:15.

"Yeah, the time is back to when I first went through it." Anna closed the door and waited. It still didn't disappear.

As Mary continued down the hallway, her mind was filled with all kinds of thoughts. What if she couldn't find them? Or what if Officer Springer made Lydia leave, and the door closed? She shook her head as if she could shake off the thoughts.

She had forgotten how oppressive the silence felt. The only sounds she could hear were her footfalls and her breath as she inhaled and exhaled. How had she withstood it for five years?

Soon, she came to the pool room. She had spent a season there: swimming, sleeping, and eating whatever showed up. She wanted to go in but felt compelled to keep walking down the main hallway.

As she walked, she thought about seeing JoJo again. Her stomach clenched. Would JoJo forgive her? It had only been five years for her, which felt like an eternity. But it had been thirty for JoJo. She grew up without a mother. Would their reunion be awkward?

Mary thought about finding her Bible on Anna's bookshelf. When she first came here, she had read a Bible she had found in the library. She studied it and prayed. When did she stop? She couldn't quite put her finger on it. But she hadn't talked to God for a long time.

She knelt on the floor and prayed.

> *Dear God, please help me find my daughter.*
> *Please help us to have a relationship again.*

She stopped, recognizing that she meant both JoJo and God. She had walked away from God without even realizing it.

Then she resumed her prayer.

Can I have a second chance, God?
Please help me to make up for the lost time.

MAX WRIGGLED and squirmed until he broke free from Dustin's arms. He jumped onto the floor and ran down the hallway. After about twenty feet, he stopped, turned his head, and looked at Anna and Dustin. Then he ran another twenty feet, sat, and looked back at them again.

"I think he wants us to follow him," Dustin said.

Anna nodded. When they walked toward him, Max continued moving down the small hallway. He kept going and going until they reached the grey room. Then Max led them past the grey room, up the main hallway, and down the smaller hallway where the second door had been. When they reached the greenhouse room, Max stopped and meowed.

"I don't think this is the time to go back in the greenhouse," Anna said.

Max looked at her and then went through a small pet door into the room. Dustin opened the door and held it open for Anna. They followed Max inside. Max had found another butterfly. He bounced and jumped as he chased it around the room.

Anna walked to the bench by the water and sat. "I guess this is as good a place as any to figure out a new plan."

Dustin nodded and sat beside her.

Anna looked around at the foliage as she listened to the soothing sound of the water gurgling and rushing through its course. As her gaze lowered, soft light reflected off a tiny object on the ground.

"Do you see that?" Anna pointed to the object. She walked over, picked it up, and turned it over in her hand.

"What is it?" he asked.

"It's an earring," she said. "I think it's my mom's earring."

Anna studied the small golden squares inset with a diamond, a sapphire, and an emerald. She remembered her mom showing her the earrings when she got them. The diamond was her birthstone, the sapphire was her mother's, and the emerald was her dad's. April, September, and May. It was delicate and beautiful.

Her mom had been here. She remembered her mom wearing them the morning she disappeared. Her mom hugged her before she got on the bus, and the earring brushed against her cheek.

"We need to find her," Anna said.

Max jumped into Dustin's lap. "Where should we start?"

"I don't know. Maybe we should pray?" She knew Dustin would think it was odd for her to suggest that. She looked at him and saw his eyes widen.

But then he closed them. He reached out and took her hand. "God," he said, "What should we do? Please help us find Anna's mom."

Before Dustin finished praying, Max jumped down and ran through the pet door. Dustin and Anna followed. As they opened the door, she saw Max sitting in the hallway, looking up at her. Then Max started toward the main hallway. They glanced at each other, shrugged their shoulders, and followed him.

CHAPTER 28

When Mary finished praying, she got up and looked around. She wasn't sure how far down the main hallway she had walked. She had passed the pool room and a few other rooms where she had spent time. But she hadn't yet made it to the music room. She was somewhere on the way in between.

She was tired. She had been walking for quite some time and needed to rest. She found a comfy-looking chair by a window and sat. When she looked at the end table, a glass of water and a yogurt parfait waited for her.

Mary smiled. Food appearing out of nowhere was the one thing about this place she missed when she went back through the door. Well, that and not having to do the dishes.

She drank some of the water. Then she picked up the parfait and gazed out the window. The flowers were so—

Her thoughts were interrupted when she felt the floor shake again. Mary started. For a moment, the pale blue sky was replaced by an expanse of stars.

She set the parfait down. The glass had tipped over, spilling water on the table. She stood and went to the window.

The shaking hadn't lasted long. And neither had the stars. But she had seen them again. She knew she had.

———

As Anna and Dustin walked toward the main hallway, the floor shook. Max yowled. They stumbled but regained their footing. Anna bent down and picked up Max.

"It's okay, Max," Anna said. "I've got you."

"This is getting to be a regular thing. It feels like our time is short."

"We're so close to the music room. Could we go? I want to hear you play something."

"This doesn't seem like a good time, Anna."

"If the place is falling apart, at least we could go out with some good music."

"Like the quartet playing as the *Titanic* sank?" he said.

"Exactly."

———

Mary continued walking down the main hallway, thinking about the stars. They were stunning. She had never seen them during her five years here. And what caused the shaking? Was it an earthquake? Or was something else happening?

She should be getting close to the music room. As she walked, she heard the faint sound of a piano. At first, it seemed like she was imagining it. But the music grew louder and louder.

The song seemed familiar. Yet, she couldn't place it. Then the music halted, a man's voice exclaimed, "Max!" and an odd combination of notes rang out.

Before she knew it, Max shot out of the room and bounded toward her. Mary smiled, reached down, and picked him up. "There you are. Lydia's going to be so happy I found you." Then Max jumped out of her arms and ran over to the man and the woman she had seen in the pictures on the fireplace mantel.

"Mom, is that you?"

"JoJo?"

Anna ran to Mary and hugged her. Mary smiled and returned the embrace.

"I never thought I'd see you again," Anna said.

Tears streamed down their cheeks.

"JoJo, I'm so sorry. I never should have gone through that door. Can you ever forgive me?"

"Oh, Mom. I already have."

Anna clung to her mom. The tears flowed as they held each other.

After a few minutes, Dustin cleared his throat. "Not to break up the reunion. But we need to get out of here."

As if on cue, a small shudder—a momentary vibration— rippled through the floor. Anna frowned. She hung onto her mom; she wasn't ready to let go. But Dustin was right. They didn't have the time she wanted.

When they separated, Mary said, "Oh, JoJo, I can't believe it. You're all grown up into a beautiful woman. I've missed so many things."

Anna reached out and ran her fingers over Mary's hair. "Your hair. It's so long. But besides that, you haven't changed. You still look so young. How is that possible?"

"I think it's only been about five years for me. Time works differently here."

"Yeah, we've noticed," Dustin said.

Anna smiled. "Oh, right, I haven't introduced you. Mom, this is my husband, Dustin. Dustin, this is my mom, Mary."

"It's nice to meet you, Dustin. I wish it were under better circumstances."

"Well, maybe it can be," Anna said.

"What do you mean?"

"We think we've found a way for you to go back."

"I've been back. I went through the door and . . ." Mary's voice trailed off.

"What is it, Mom?"

"Oh, JoJo, how can I tell you?" Mary shut her eyes and shook her head. "I was the one who shut the door. It's my fault you were trapped here."

Mary recounted how she had found the door again, how she saw them without knowing who they were, how she closed the door without thinking, and how she had been trying to figure out a way to fix everything.

Max circled Mary's legs and sat by her right foot. Mary picked him up and rubbed his ears. "And little Max, here—"

"You know about Max?" Anna asked.

"Oh, yes. Lydia came over. We've been spending time together, waiting for the door to return."

"She can see the door?"

"She's on the other side, making sure it stays open."

"Oh, Mom, when I said that we've found a way for you to go back, I meant back to the day you left."

"What?" Mary raised her eyebrows and tilted her head. "But how? We can't go back in time. Can we?"

"We found another door."

"There are other doors?"

"It goes back to the day you left—after you were gone but before I came home from school. And since you look the same as when you left—besides your hair—I think it might work."

"Do you think it's still there?"

"This door's different. As far as we could tell, it's always there."

As they talked, a deep boom resounded through the hallway. The floor seemed to convulse. Anna lost her footing, fell, and hit her head on the wall. She heard Mary scream, and then she blacked out.

CHAPTER 29

A nna felt a dull ache in her elbow. She tried to discern what was causing it. And then she realized she was lying with her arm scrunched under her. She rolled onto her right side and freed her left arm. The ache subsided, replaced by needle-like stings.

She felt a soft sandpaper tongue on the back of her hand. She tried to open her eyes, but they burned. As her eyes watered, she was able to open them a little. She saw Max sitting beside her. Dust floated in the air, and the floor was covered with debris.

"What happened, Max?" She pulled him toward her and held him close. After she regained some strength, she sat up and looked around her.

Mary lay several feet away and began to stir.

"Mom? Are you okay?"

"I think so," Mary said. "I just need a moment."

Anna looked for Dustin. When she didn't see him, her heart raced. She called out his name.

"I'm over here."

The sound of his voice calmed her. She turned and saw

him sitting up. The dust started to settle. Dustin stood and walked to Anna.

"Are you alright?" he asked. "Does anything hurt?"

"I hit my head, but I think I'm alright."

"Did you lose consciousness?"

"Maybe for a minute." He took her hands and pulled her up. Then he went to Mary and helped her to her feet.

"What happened?" Anna asked.

"I'm not sure," Dustin said. "It must have been a big meteor."

"Meteor?" Mary said. "What do you mean?"

Dustin explained how they were in the room with the skylight, how they had seen the small meteors hit the glass, and how one of them broke through. As he talked, Anna watched the hallway—well, clean itself up was the best way she could describe it. The dust and debris were gone.

Mary's eyes widened. "I saw stars."

Anna put her arm around her mom. "Yeah, so did we." Then Anna looked out the window. The view wavered between green hills and stars. Anna pointed. "Look."

Dustin and Mary turned to look through the window. There were stars, then green hills, and then stars again. After a few moments, the view stayed fixed on the rolling green hills and wildflowers under the pale blue sky.

"I think we need to get Mary to the third door," Dustin said. "The quicker the better."

"How did you find the other door?" Mary asked.

"It was on a map we found."

"Can I see it?"

"Let's go over there so I can spread it out," Dustin said.

Anna and Mary followed Dustin to a table. Anna held Max close to her as his body trembled.

Dustin rolled out Charles's map. He showed Mary where they were, where the Big Kitchen was, and the locations of the other two doors.

Mary leaned forward and ran her hand over the map. "Where did you find it?"

"In an old desk," Anna said. She explained how they found the desk and the letter Charles wrote to Margaret. Then she said, "On the day you went missing, I saw a man run out of our house."

"I know. Lydia told me. I'm so sorry you were scared and that I wasn't there for you."

"It's okay, Mom. I only brought it up because we think Charles was the man I saw."

"Yeah, when Lydia told me, I wondered if the man you saw was how I got trapped in here. When he went through the door, he must have closed it."

Anna looked at Mary and smiled. "I wish we had more time to sit and talk."

"I wish you had more time, too," Dustin said. "But we'd better get going."

They walked down the main hallway, looking for the smaller one. When they reached the place where it should have been, it was blocked. The grey room was still on their right. But on their left, a large rock had breached the ceiling and penetrated the floor. The rock was black and smooth— the same texture as the smaller stony-iron that went through the table.

Anna looked up. The ceiling had healed itself around the rock, and the rock was intertwined with the fabric of the space. When she looked down, the floor was the same. There was no debris or dust to suggest its entry. And it didn't look like there was an opening around it. The rock closed off the hallway as effectively as a steel door.

"I guess we're not going this way," Anna said. She watched as Dustin looked it over from every angle.

"There isn't any way around or over it," he said. "Let me look at the map again."

Dustin found a table and opened the map. "To enter the

hallway from the other side, we could go around the bottom curve. Or we could take the hallway by the music room. I think it's a little shorter to go back by the music room."

"Who was playing the piano right before I found you?" Mary asked.

"That was Dustin," Anna said. "I have no musical talent. Doesn't he sound amazing?"

"I didn't see a piano in your house."

"I've been telling Dustin how we should get one."

THEY WALKED BACK up the main hallway. Max had stopped shivering. He jumped out of Anna's arms and led the way. Soon, they reached the music room.

"Here's where we turn right." Max rounded the corner like he understood what Dustin said.

"I know time is running out," Anna said. "But could we rest for a minute? I'm feeling a little dizzy."

"Are you okay?" Dustin took her arm as they walked into the music room. "Here, sit down until the dizziness subsides."

"Maybe you could play something for us?" Anna smiled at him. "Please?"

"Fine."

Mary sat by Anna. There was a pitcher of water and some glasses on the coffee table. A bowl of water was on the floor for Max. Mary poured some water for Anna and handed it to her. Then she poured some for herself.

Dustin played a piece by Johann Sebastian Bach: *Prelude No. 1 in C Major*. The music filled the room. Anna rested her eyes. Before she knew it, the song was over.

"How are you feeling?" Dustin asked. "Are you still dizzy?"

Anna opened her eyes. "I think it's gone now. Maybe I just needed some water."

He helped her off the couch. "We better keep going."

THEY WALKED up the smaller hallway. When Anna could see the greenhouse ahead, she remembered the earring she had found. She reached into her pocket and pulled it out.

"Look what I found, Mom."

"Oh, JoJo. I thought I lost that for good." Mary reached into her pocket and pulled out the other one. "Now I have them both again. Where was it?" she asked as she put them on.

"I found it in the greenhouse, back by the pond."

"It's beautiful in there, isn't it?"

Max ran ahead and shot through the pet door. "Max," Anna shouted. "We don't have time for you to play in the greenhouse."

Just then, Max bounded back through the pet door. Somehow, a butterfly had escaped with him. He chased it up the hallway.

Anna laughed. "At least he's going in the right direction now."

CHAPTER 30

"Hey, Dusty," Anna said. "Do you think we have time to show my mom the second door?"

"Anna, I don't know. We should keep moving."

"It will only take a minute." Anna pointed out the icebox and the mahogany door with the intricate doorknob. "We think this is the door from Charles's time. Have you seen it before?"

"I've been to the greenhouse," Mary said. "But I don't remember. I might have walked by without noticing it."

Dustin gave Anna a we-need-to-get-going look. But Anna was enjoying the time with her mom. She glanced at him and shrugged.

"Did you try opening it?" Mary asked.

"It's locked." Anna reached out and twisted the doorknob. It still didn't open. "Before we suspected it was Charles's door, we tried to guess where it might lead." She smiled at Mary. "My vote was for Paris."

Mary's face seemed to light up. "I wonder . . ."

"What is it, Mom?"

Mary reached into her pocket and pulled out a key. "I found this in your dining room. It's probably not the right one. But it couldn't hurt to try."

Anna studied the antique key. She ran her fingers over the choppy edges of the puzzle-piece-like end. Then she put it in the lock, turned it counter-clockwise, and heard a small click. She grinned at Mary and looked back at Dustin. "It worked."

"Anna, we don't have time to go exploring. We need to get your mom to the other door."

As if she didn't hear, Anna turned the intricate brass knob and opened the door a crack. She continued opening the door incrementally, stopping each time to study what she saw. When she didn't see anyone, she opened it wide and stepped through.

She stood and listened. The only sound she heard was the crackling of a fire. She looked over her shoulder and saw Dustin mouth, *What are you doing?* In response, she motioned for him to follow her.

Mary entered next. "Dustin said he's going to keep an eye on the door so we don't get stuck here."

"Isn't this amazing?" Anna said. "It's like it has the same bones as our house. But it's so different."

They stood in silence, taking it in. In the middle of the far wall stood a cast-iron wood-burning stove. The stove's pedestal and doors were pressed with decorative designs. Steam rose from a teapot on one of its burners. A large black pipe came out of the top of the stove and curved into the wall. And beside the stove was a water heater.

By another wall sat an icebox like the one they had seen before they came through the door. Next to it, a large porcelain sink was surrounded by freestanding cabinets with open shelving and cupboards. Cast iron pots and skillets hung on a large metal apparatus over an island with a wooden countertop in the middle of the room. Through a door in the corner, she saw a large pantry lined with jars of food.

Floor tiles surrounded the stove, and the remaining floor was wood. White wainscotting skirted the bottom half of the walls. Sunlight filtered through several windows. There weren't any electric lights.

Anna walked to one of the windows. She saw a small oak tree in the backyard and a large garden farther back. There was no sign of Mrs. Garwood's house. The countryside stretched out as far as she could see.

"It's pretty unbelievable," Mary said. She pointed to the stove. "Could you imagine cooking on that?"

Anna shook her head. "Yeah, and there's no dishwasher, refrigerator, or microwave. Let's see what it looks like down the hallway."

"I don't think we should stay much longer."

"It will only take a second."

As Anna walked, she noted the differences. Instead of a living room, there was a large dining area. An ornate birchwood table extended through the room. She counted fourteen chairs. She stepped into the room and ran her hand over the table. The wavy grain of the reddish-brown wood felt smooth under her fingertips.

A matching sideboard filled with bone-white china stood on one side of the room—the edges of each plate decorated with a delicate floral pattern. On the other side, a large hearth had been prepared for a fire. Light shining through a gap in the heavy drapes revealed flowery paper on the walls.

She returned to the hallway. Through the next doorway, she saw a den. And through a third, a drawing room with an upright piano in one corner. She went back to the den. As she walked through the door, a lion's face stared at her from the corner of the desk.

"It's exactly like the desk where we found Charles's map," Anna said.

The staring lion, the roaring lion, the closed-mouth lion, and the regal lion were all there. Anna ran her hand over the cherry wood and the grapevine carving. Then she saw the keyhole. She reached into her left pocket. The key to the other desk was still there.

"Watch this," she said. She put the key in the keyhole and turned it. The drawer on the right side of the desk popped out.

She pulled out the drawer. Like the drawer on the other desk, it was long and rectangular. She felt inside the drawer with her right hand while holding it with her left. The drawer was empty, but her hand brushed against a small round piece of wood on the top. It was smooth, unlike the unfinished drawer. When she pressed on it, a miniature desk popped up from the center of the larger one.

The small desk had two little drawers on either side. She pulled on one of the knobs, barely larger than the head of a pin. It was an actual drawer that came all the way out. Three of the tiny drawers were empty. But a fourth contained a ring.

She turned the drawer over, and the ring fell into her palm. It was a large emerald set on a band of gold.

"Look, Mom. It must be for Margaret."

"Wow, it's such a deep green."

"Isn't it beautiful?"

Anna stopped talking when she heard a whistling sound. The teapot was ready. Then, she heard footsteps. "It sounds like someone's coming down the staircase," she whispered.

Mary gripped Anna's hand. It was shaking.

"We'd better go," Mary said.

Anna put the ring back into the drawer. She had trouble fitting it back into its place on the small desk. At last, she was able to line up the drawer and close it. She pushed the small desk down into the bigger one, and the wood on the desk moved back into place. They hurried out of the room and down the hallway.

"I'll be right behind you," Anna said. "I need to do something first."

Anna reached into her back pocket and pulled out the letter. She unfolded it and smoothed it out the best she could. Then she set it on the island and followed Mary through the door.

Dustin shut the door behind them, locked it, and handed the key to Mary. "Let's go."

"Don't you want to hear about what was in there?" Anna asked.

"There's no time," he said.

"Wait, where's Max?" Anna looked around but didn't see him. "You don't think he slipped by us into Charles's house, do you?"

"I didn't see him," Mary said. "But I was pretty focused on the old stove and everything."

"What if he's in there, Dustin? We can't leave him in 1901."

"Anna's right. Lydia would be devastated."

Dustin sighed. "I guess you'd better look."

Mary handed Anna the key. Anna unlocked it and cautiously opened it. When she didn't see anyone, she stepped through. Steam rose from the teapot, but it wasn't whistling yet. She looked around the kitchen and called his name. The table where she set the letter was empty.

She walked up the hallway. She searched the rooms but didn't see him. There was no sign of Max in the dining room or the den. Then the teapot started to whistle, and the stairs creaked as someone descended them.

She ran back to the door. After she looked behind her, she stepped through, closed the door, and locked it. "I didn't see Max. I think this door might be on a time loop like the other one."

"A time loop?" Mary asked.

"Every time the door closes," Anna said, "it resets the time."

Mary nodded even though her face looked blank.

"If the time loop reset," Dustin said, "you wouldn't be able to find him. He would be moving forward on the timeline he stepped into."

"Like a multiverse?" Anna asked.

"Yes."

"I'm not sure I understand," Mary said.

Anna slumped onto a couch close to the door. Her mind was troubled at the thought of Max being trapped in 1901. Why hadn't she been more careful? She sighed. She should have made sure someone was holding Max before she opened the door.

Mary sat beside her and took her hand. "Don't worry, JoJo. We'll figure it out."

"I should have been watching him."

"We all should have."

"What if we don't find him?"

The floor shook. This time, the shaking lasted for almost a minute.

"I know we don't want to leave Max behind," Dustin said. "But the reality is that we need to get moving."

Anna frowned. Then she heard it: a faint cry and a *thwap*. "Did you hear that?"

"Hear what?" Dustin asked.

She tilted her head and listened. Another cry; another *thwap*. It was coming from somewhere up the hallway.

Anna stood and walked toward the sound. The cry and the *thwap* grew louder. And then she saw the corner of the pet door open. A cry escaped before it closed with a *thwap*.

She called to Dustin and Mary. Then she opened the door to the greenhouse, and Max sprinted out. He ran down the hallway and back to Anna.

"I should have known you'd go back in there. Did you find another butterfly?"

Max bounced and mewed. She picked him up and headed toward Dustin and Mary.

"Hey, look who I found."

Dustin and Mary smiled.

"Okay," Dustin said, "let's go."

CHAPTER 31

As they resumed their journey toward the third door, Max jumped out of Anna's arms. At times, he walked out in front. Other times, he circled, almost like he was herding them.

Mary asked Anna how she met Dustin. Anna told her the story of how she had been walking on DU's campus with her coffee in one hand while she was looking at a class syllabus in the other, how she ran into him and spilled her coffee on his shirt, and how they had been inseparable ever since. Then she described their wedding in detail.

"It was in Aspen, in late May—outdoors on a sunny day. There was just a hint of snow left on the mountains with wild-flowers blooming in the distance."

"What colors did you choose?"

"Different shades of blush, cream, and white. My bouquet was made of pale pink and white roses and white peonies."

"That sounds beautiful."

"Oh, Mom, it was. You would have loved it." Anna looked over and saw tears falling down Mary's cheeks. "I didn't mean to make you cry." She reached out and hugged her mom.

"Before he walked me down the aisle, Dad told me there was no way you'd miss it if you could help it."

"He was right. I so wish I could have been there."

"Do you hear that?" Dustin asked.

"I don't hear anything," Anna said.

"Listen."

They stopped walking. Max mewed. Without their feet shuffling, Anna heard the faint sound of music. "It sounds like—"

"Ballroom music?" Mary said.

"Yeah," Anna said. "That's it." The music was lively.

"It's coming from that room up ahead," Dustin said.

Anna walked to the doorway of the room. "It looks like a grand dining hall." She walked into the room, and the others followed.

The room was bright with ornate crown molding, columns, and designs engraved on the ivory-colored walls. Candlelit chandeliers were evenly spaced throughout the room, and a stained-glass dome dispersed a gentle light through the space. Large vases with white lilies were positioned around the sides.

Half of the room had round tables adorned with linen tablecloths, fine china, crystal, and silver. The china was bone-white with hints of a bright blue floral pattern. The other half of the room had an empty marble floor waiting for the dancers to arrive.

When Anna saw that Mary was walking through the room, taking it all in, she went over to Dustin. "I would like to spend more time with my mom. Could we sit down for dinner?"

Dustin rubbed the back of his neck. "I'm not sure."

"Please? There haven't been any tremors for a while."

"That's true." He sighed as he tilted his head from side to side. "Yeah, I guess the meteor shower must be over. I think it would be okay."

She smiled and kissed him on the cheek. "Thanks for understanding." Anna walked over to Mary.

"Look at this," Mary said. "It has nameplates with our names on them."

In the middle of the table, she saw a platter of roast prime ribs of beef and bowls of steamed potatoes with cream, cauliflower au gratin, and a salad with French dressing. To the side were baked apple dumplings for dessert.

"Let's sit down," Anna said. "It looks amazing." As she sat, Anna looked down. Small bowls of food and water were on the floor. "Look," Anna said, "Max has salmon. He's going to get spoiled."

"I think he's already spoiled," Mary said.

Anna smiled. Mary gave thanks. They all said amen and passed around the platter and bowls.

"These potatoes are delicious," Anna said. Then she took a sip of the lemonade.

"Remember our California trip?" Mary asked. She pulled the old photo out of her pocket and handed it to Anna. "I found this on your fireplace mantel. It helped me to figure out what was going on when I went back through the door."

"I love that picture." Anna looked at Mary in the photo. "You know, you really do look the same as the day you went through the door."

"You were so excited to go to the beach," Mary said. "You talked about it for weeks before we went, asking me every day when we would go."

"I remember Dad doing backflips on the beach. I tried to do one but all I could do was a cartwheel."

"We laughed so much on that trip," Mary said.

"Yeah, we did."

Anna told Mary about some of the milestones in her life. It was a joyous time of conversation and laughter. Though every so often, they felt a small tremor, which made ripples in their lemonade.

"Where did you grow up, Dustin?"

"It wasn't far from your house," he said. "It was west, maybe five miles."

"Yeah, can you believe it?" Anna said. "We lived so close to each other for all those years and never knew it until we met at DU."

Perhaps wanting to join the fun, Max jumped into Anna's lap. He seemed to size everything up, looking to his right and left. Then he jumped across the table, landing on Dustin's chest. Everyone laughed.

"Owww! Easy on the claws, Max." Dustin took Max's paws off his chest and turned him around.

"Max steals the show once again," Anna said.

"Yeah, he's a regular—"

As the music hit a high note, the floor lurched. The bowl of potatoes slid off the table and crashed onto the floor.

"We need to get Mary to the door," Dustin said. "Now!"

They got up and headed for the hallway. In front of them, the marble floor buckled. Mary shrieked and pointed at Max. Anna looked down and saw Dustin pick Max up just before the floor gave way beneath his paws.

Then one of the chandeliers fell to the floor and shattered. The small crystal ovals were propelled through the room, and Anna heard one as it shot past her ear.

As they ran out into the hallway, a piece of the ceiling fractured and collapsed a few feet in front of them. Max howled. They stopped and held onto the wall as the floor continued shaking.

Anna closed her eyes. When the tremors stopped, she opened them. It was hazy. She squeezed her eyes shut and then blinked rapidly. Her eyes watered, irritated by the dust in the air. When her eyes could focus, she realized that a pile of rubble blocked the way.

"Is everyone okay?" Dustin asked.

Anna watched Mary nod. Stunned, she also nodded. No words came.

She watched and waited for the hallway to heal itself. It didn't. The damage remained, and the dust slowly settled. Why wasn't it putting itself back together?

CHAPTER 32

Dustin handed Max to Anna. "I'm going to try to find a way around the debris."

Anna took Max in her arms and rubbed his head. She watched Dustin enter the bedroom closest to the wreckage on their left. After a moment, he came out.

"There's not another exit from that one."

Then Dustin went into the bedroom on their right. Anna heard a door open, something fall on the floor, and the door slam.

When Dustin came out, he said, "That one had a second doorway. But it's in the middle of the rubble."

Dustin walked along the wall of debris—pulling on it, standing on his toes, reaching, and crouching. Toward Anna's left, he put his hands on something, pulled his body up, and disappeared. A few minutes later, he reappeared the way he had left.

"I think I found a way to get through it," he said. "It won't be easy. We'll have to crawl. But I don't see another way."

"How far will we have to crawl?" Anna asked.

"About eighteen to twenty feet."

Mary cringed.

"What's wrong, Mom?"

"How are we going to get up there? I can't pull myself up like Dustin did."

"Yeah, I don't think I can either," Anna said.

"Maybe we can find a chair or something," Dustin said.

Anna turned and walked up the hallway. Some of the pictures had fallen off the wall. She went back into the dining room. One of the columns had collapsed. She looked at the floor as she walked, stepping around the places where the floor had caved in. The chairs were overturned, lying this way and that. She held Max in one arm and dragged a chair with the other.

After lugging it through the rubble, she managed to make it out of the dining room and into the hallway. "Will this work?" she asked.

"I found a step stool in that kitchen over there," Dustin said.

"Why didn't you say something?"

"I was just about to."

"Let's not waste time arguing," Mary said. "We may need them both."

Dustin walked to where he had found the opening. He cleared some drywall from the floor, positioned the step stool under the opening, and climbed the steps. Then he pushed down on a steel beam sticking out from the debris about five feet from the floor. It didn't move. He looked up, put his hands around a second beam above the first, and hung from it for a moment. It didn't move either.

He eased back down onto the stool. Then he put his foot on the first beam, his left foot on the second one, and climbed into the small passageway. He turned around and said, "It's narrow. I can only help one at a time because you won't have room to go around me. Who wants to go first?"

"You go first, Mom."

"Oh no, JoJo. You go first. I insist."

Anna climbed the steps on the stool and handed Max to Dustin.

"Watch out for this edge," Dustin said. He pointed at a piece of metal sticking out of the pile. "It's sharp."

She put her foot on the first beam like she had watched Dustin do. But when she attempted to put her left foot on the second beam, it slipped. She yelped.

Dustin caught her hand. "You're okay." He steadied her until she could put her feet back on the two beams. She climbed up the rest of the way. When she reached the top, Dustin crawled forward into the small tunnel, making room for her.

"Are you ready?" he asked.

"No, but let's go anyway." Anna looked down at Mary. "See you in a few minutes, Mom."

Anna crawled behind Dustin. As they moved forward, it grew dark. At first, she felt smooth metal, then splintered wood, then pieces of drywall, and then metal again. Before long, the light filtered through again, and they reached the other side.

Dustin handed Max to Anna. "I'm going to find a way to climb down. Then you can hand Max to me."

She watched Dustin navigate the debris. When he was a few feet off the floor, he jumped down. "I'll be right back."

He disappeared for several minutes. She heard Mary shout, "Is everything okay?"

"He's trying to find a chair or something."

Then she saw him carrying a large dining room chair. He put it below her and stood on it.

"Here, hand Max to me."

Anna reached down and dropped Max. Dustin caught him. Max yowled.

"I know, Max, it's not the high point of your day." Dustin got off the chair and set Max on the floor. "Okay, your turn."

Anna looked over the edge of the debris and tried to see how to climb down. "How? I don't see a way."

Dustin pointed at a beam. "See this? Turn your body around and set your foot on the beam. Then I'll be able to help you down."

Anna's heart raced. She shifted her body but stopped. "I can't do it."

"Yes, you can. I'm right here."

She held her breath as she slowly turned and extended her foot. "I don't feel it."

Dustin reached up and guided her foot. "You're just a few inches above it. Trust me."

Anna let go and landed on the beam. She looked down at Dustin.

He pointed again. "Now grab right there with your left hand and ease down onto the chair."

As she followed his directions, he reached up, put his arms around her, and lowered her to the floor.

"See," he said, "you did great."

"It would've been easier if someone could have dropped me into your arms like we did with Max."

Dustin smiled. "I need to get your mom." Dustin got on the chair, reached up, held onto the beam, and lifted himself to the passageway.

"He makes it look so easy, Max." Anna bent down and scratched Max's ears.

As she waited, she heard Dustin's voice but couldn't make out what he was saying. Then the debris creaked. Finally, she saw Dustin's head pop out of the small tunnel, and he climbed down.

MARY INCHED along in the darkness, following the outline of Dustin's form. The textures beneath her hands and knees alternated between cold metal, splintered wood, and irregular pieces of drywall. She winced and cried out in pain. A small, hard piece of debris had found its way under the patella of her knee as she moved forward.

"Are you okay?" Dustin asked.

"Yes. It was a pebble in my knee. I'm fine now."

She saw the light up ahead. At last, she saw Dustin making his way down.

Anna watched Dustin climb down. "Where's my mom?"

"She was right behind me."

"Oh look, there she is."

Just as Mary's head emerged from the passageway, the debris squealed as it shifted. Mary screamed and disappeared.

"Mom!" Anna shouted.

CHAPTER 33

Dustin scrambled up to the opening and reached into the hole. "Mary?"

"I'm okay. I think. Can you grab my hand?"

"I can't see it," he said.

Anna's heart felt like it had dropped into her stomach. "Mom? Are you okay?"

"I think something is on my foot. I can't get it free."

MARY REACHED DOWN and felt bands of metal around her foot. It was like her foot was in a cage. She could move it around, but she couldn't pull it out. A feeling of dread washed over her; it felt like she couldn't catch her breath.

Then she saw Dustin crawling toward her. "Are you hurt?"

"No, I just can't get my foot out. There's metal all around it."

His eyebrows narrowed. "Let me think for a moment."

Mary tried to slow her breathing as she waited. Her hip was cramping. "Maybe you and Anna should go. If I can't get free, then at least you'll make it home safely."

"I heard that," Anna shouted. "We're not leaving without you."

"Yeah, what she said. Can you move the metal at all?"

"No," Mary said. "I tried. It won't budge."

ANNA CLEARED a space on the floor and sat with her legs crossed. Max hopped into her lap.

"Hold tight," Dustin said. "I'm going to think of a way to get you free."

She looked up and saw Dustin climbing down the pile. When he was on the floor, he walked toward her.

"I'm not sure what I can do." He whispered so Mary couldn't hear him. "I can't get into the tunnel to even look at her foot. It's too narrow."

He paced, paused, and then paced again. As she watched him, she felt a soft paw bat at her necklace. She watched the small cross as it swung. "Good idea, Max. Why didn't I think of praying?"

She closed her eyes. "God, please help us. Please help my mom get free. I don't think you would have brought us this far to let it end like this."

As she prayed, the floor began to tremble again. There was another squeal, and the pile shifted.

"I'm free," Mary shouted.

Anna pressed her palm over her heart. *Thank you, God.* When she looked up, she saw her mom's face as she exited the tunnel. Above her was a light and a brief glimpse of something like the face of a man. She blinked, and it was gone.

DUSTIN HELPED Mary climb down the pile. When she was on

the floor, Anna sprang up and went over to her. "Is your foot alright? Which one was it?"

"It was this one, but it's fine." Anna crouched and examined Mary's foot. Large gouges marred the sole of her shoe, but none went all the way through.

Anna stood and hugged her mom. "I'm so glad you're okay." As she said it, the floor trembled.

"Let's get going," Dustin said.

Soon, Anna could see where the hallway teed off into the one that went down to Charles's desk. "Look, we're almost to the end of this hallway."

When they reached the end, they turned right. Anna saw furniture overturned in every room. Chairs had been cast away from the tables and lay on their sides. The floor had given way in places, and some walls had crumbled.

Out the windows, she saw the view fluctuating between the rolling green hills and stars. When the rolling green hills were there, a soft light filtered through the windows. But when they were replaced with stars, it was darker. It had a strobe-like effect as it alternated between the two.

She bent down to put Max on the floor, but he resisted and clung to her. "I think Max can sense the danger."

"Is he okay?" Dustin asked.

"Let's just say that he's clingy."

The tremors were increasing in frequency. Every minute or so, the floor shook.

"We're running out of time," Dustin said. "Let's pick up the pace."

They walked in silence. As they reached the hallway that led to the third door, Anna looked up and saw Charles's desk. She handed Max to Mary. "I'll be right back," she said.

"We don't have time for that," Dustin said. But Anna had already started running toward the desk.

As she approached it, one of the lion's heads seemed to look at her with disapproval. She reached into her pocket and pulled out the key. The ground shook, and she steadied her hand to line it up with the keyhole. She turned the key, and the drawer popped out of the side like before.

She reached down and felt the top where the drawer had come out. Like the one she found in Charles's house, she felt a smooth, round piece of wood. When she pressed it, the miniature desk popped up from the center of the larger one.

Anna opened the fourth tiny drawer and gasped. There was the emerald ring. She pulled the drawer out, dumped the ring into her hand, and sprinted back to the others.

As Anna ran toward Dustin and Mary, the verse from her fortune cookie came into her mind.

Whoever has no rule over his own spirit is like
a city broken down, without walls.

She remembered learning in Sunday school how cities in Biblical times had walls around them to protect everyone inside. She cringed a little as she realized that her lack of self-control had put them all in danger—more than once. What if they wouldn't be able to get her mom safely to the door because of what she had done?

"Anna, why did you——"

"I know, I know. I'm sorry. I put us all at risk. It was reckless to run off like that. I don't know what came over me. I felt compelled to look. But I shouldn't have gone."

Dustin looked surprised.

"But look at what I found." She handed the ring to Dustin. "We saw one just like it when we went through the second door. It was in Charles's den. We think he got it for Maggie."

"It's beautiful. But a ring isn't worth your life." He handed it back to Anna.

"You're right." Anna gave the ring to Mary. "I want you to take it with you, Mom."

"Oh, Anna, I couldn't. You should keep it."

"Please, Mom. I can't explain it, but I think you'll need it."

"Let's go," Dustin said. "In case you forgot, this place is falling apart."

CHAPTER 34

As they walked toward the third door, the shaking increased in frequency. The tremors lasted longer and were more intense. Destruction was all around them. They zigzagged around the rubble they encountered in the hallway like they were moving through an obstacle course.

At last, Anna saw the third door ahead. "Look, there it is."

They walked into the kitchen and stood by the door with the brass knob.

"Do you hear that?" Dustin asked.

"It sounds like something frying in a pan," Mary said.

Anna looked at the stove. There was nothing there. But when she turned, she saw a skillet of beef fajitas on the table behind them. One moment, sizzles and pops came from the skillet. Steam rose, carrying the smell of onions and peppers frying. The next moment, it was gone. But the fragrant mist hung in the air, seemingly without a source.

The next instant, the table was set with freshly made tortillas and small bowls of rice, black beans, guacamole, pico, sour cream, and cheese. The floor shook, and the bowl of beans slid off the table and smashed onto the floor as the rest of the bowls disappeared.

The floor lurched. Anna fell forward, and Dustin caught her. As she regained her footing, she frowned.

Anna reached out and took Mary's hand. "I don't want you to go. I mean, I do. But . . ." Anna's thoughts seemed to run wild. Would this door lead her mom into a different timeline? Were there an infinite number of lives for each one of them? How could they be sure everything would be restored when Mary went through the door?

Mary squeezed her hand. "What is it, JoJo?"

"What if it is like a multiverse, so the Anna on the other side of this door gets to grow up with her mom—you. But I go home and never see you again. What if we'll be on two different timelines?" Anna looked at her feet. "It feels like I'm losing you all over again."

Mary pulled Anna close and hugged her. "Oh, JoJo. I don't think there's more than one universe. God created one of you and one of me. And He's able to straighten it all out. He delights in you. You can trust Him."

Anna nodded. "I still don't want to let you go. I just got you back."

Mary squeezed her tightly as the floor heaved again.

"It's time," Dustin said. "We need to get Mary through the door." He held Max tightly.

Mary kissed Anna's cheek. "Remember, God can do what we can't even imagine. Never forget how much I love you."

"I love you, Mom."

Mary turned the brass knob, opened the door, and stepped through.

Anna watched the door close. This time, it disappeared into the wall. And when she looked at Withers's *The Road Home*, she was certain the woman had decided to turn around and go back to her family.

Anna ran up the smaller hallway with Max tucked under her left arm like a football. Dustin was at her side. The shaking was continuous now. Out each window, the stars spread out into what seemed like infinity. She wanted to stop and stare at their marvelous beauty. But there was no time.

With her right hand, she clutched the small, gold cross pendant her mom had given her. *God, please help us to make it home.*

The silence had been replaced by a rushing wind and the sound of metal, wood, and tile breaking apart. Debris shot past them as they ran. She let go of the cross pendant and reached for Dustin's hand.

They sprinted, hand-in-hand, up the hallway. At last, she saw the room with the exercise bikes, then the small kitchen where they had eaten lunch, and then the perfectly square bedroom.

Finally, the Big Kitchen came into view on their right. As they ran past it, she saw Mrs. Garwood in the open doorway. Mrs. Garwood smiled and waved. Anna took one last look at Monet's *The Road to Chailly*. Then they leaped through the open doorway.

The instant they were through the door, it shut behind them as the Big Kitchen disintegrated into space.

CHAPTER 35
THIRTY YEARS EARLIER

Mary looked around her. Everything was just as she remembered. There was the red phone. There, the calendar proclaimed it to be 1991. Her purse was on the counter. The big clock hung on the wall over the kitchen table. And there was the wall separating the kitchen from the living room. She opened the garage door and saw her car parked inside.

The phone startled her when it rang. She picked it up but didn't say anything. Then she heard, "Hello? Is there anyone there?" It was Lydia. For some reason, she froze. No words came. Then Lydia said, "Mary? Mary dear, is that you? Are you home?"

Mary hung up the phone. Tears streamed down her face. Why hadn't she spoken?

She walked around the familiar house: looking, touching, waiting. What time did Anna say she would get home? 3:30? It was only 3:20. She still had a few minutes.

She went over to the fireplace mantel. The picture of her, Jim, and JoJo smiling as the sun set behind them sat there in the frame she had broken. The glass was intact again. She reached into the patch pocket of her sweater but didn't feel the photo. It was gone.

She hurried up the steps into the bathroom and looked in the mirror. Her face was smudged with dirt and grime. She washed it and wondered if she should cut her hair. But there wasn't enough time. She found a hair tie in the back of the drawer and thought about putting her hair in a ponytail. She decided against it and went downstairs into the kitchen.

At times, minutes can drag on like hours. Now was one of those times. Should she go onto the front porch and wait? At last, she heard Anna rush through the front door and call out for her.

"I'm in the kitchen, JoJo."

She heard Anna's footsteps as she ran down the hallway. Then she saw Anna's golden pigtails bouncing as she ran toward her and into her outstretched arms. *Thank you, God, for giving me a second chance. Please help me not to take it for granted.* She held Anna tightly. Mary's cheeks were wet with tears.

"What's wrong, Mommy?"

"I'm just so happy to see you."

Mary looked up at Lydia and smiled. A few white strands stood out in her friend's chestnut brown hair. She felt JoJo's small arms wrap around her neck, and her hands ran down her hair.

"Wow, your hair is so long," Anna said. Then, pulling away, she scrunched up her face and asked, "Who was the man who ran out of our house?"

A NOTE FROM THE AUTHOR

"I am the door. If anyone enters by Me,
he will be saved . . . ." (John 10:9)

Have you gone through the door yet? Not a magical one like in this story, but the one made by Jesus when He died on the cross for your sins. If you haven't, you can right now.

If you want to go through the door, follow these steps:

1. *Admit that you've fallen short of God's perfect standard.*

"[F]or all have sinned and fall short of the glory of God." (Romans 3:23)

2. *Acknowledge the cost of your sin.*

"For the wages of sin is death . . . ." (Romans 6:23a)

3. *Know how much God loves you.*

"But God demonstrates His own love toward us, in that while we were still sinners, Christ died for us." (Romans 5:8)

"For God so loved the world that He gave His only begotten Son, that whoever believes in Him should not perish but have everlasting life." (John 3:16)

4. *Recognize what you will gain by accepting God's gift.*

"[B]ut the gift of God is eternal life in Christ Jesus our Lord." (Romans 6:23b)

5. *Accept God's free gift.*

"[I]f you confess with your mouth the Lord Jesus and believe in your heart that God has raised Him from the dead, you will be saved. . . . For 'whoever calls on the name of the LORD shall be saved.'" (Romans 10:9, 13 (quoting Joel 2:32))

Here's a prayer you can use to help you talk to God. The specific words aren't important—God's more concerned with your heart. But these words may help you to confess that Jesus is Lord.

Dear God, I know that I've sinned and need Your forgiveness. Thank You for sending Your Son, Jesus, to die on the cross for my sins. I believe that He lived, died, and came to life again. Please forgive my sins and help me to obey and follow You for the rest of my life. I want Jesus to be Lord over my life. In Jesus' name, amen.

If you have confessed with your mouth the Lord Jesus and believe in your heart that God has raised Him from the dead, you've been born again into God's family (John 1:12). I encourage you to read your Bible and pray every day. As you do, you'll learn more about who God is and how He wants you to live.

ALSO BY CATHERINE MCDAUGALE

NONFICTION BOOKS

Ebenezer Stones: using an ordinary stone to remind you of our extraordinary God

Ebenezer Stones Study Guide

How to Teach Your Kids about God

www.ingramcontent.com/pod-product-compliance
Lightning Source LLC
Chambersburg PA
CBHW032222190726
48289CB00007BA/2350